I0548288

aHunter4Life

By

Cynthia A Clement

Text copyright © 2014 Cynthia A Clement

Book Edition
ISBN: 978-0-9938457-1-0

All Rights Reserved. No part of this publication may be reproduced, stored in, or introduced into a retrieval system, or transmitted in any form, or by any means (electronic, mechanical, photocopying, recording, or otherwise) without prior written permission of the copyright owner and publisher. For the purposes of a reviewer, brief passages may be quoted in a review to be printed in a newspaper, magazine, or journal.

This book is a work of fiction. The characters and incidents are from the author's imagination. Any resemblance to actual incidents or persons, living or dead, is coincidental and unintentional.

Book Cover designed by RomCon®
Cover Image: Jenn LeBlanc / Illustrated Romance

Dedication

To my editing team. Thanks to you, lair is not liar.

Chapter 1

She was near.

Deep in his bones, her essence surrounded him. The memory of her was an ache that eight long years had not dulled. His head spun with the possibilities of what this meant. His breath caught in his throat; he forced himself to exhale. He'd been frantic to find her, but his efforts had been futile. She chose this moment, when he was on assignment in Beverly Hills, to reach out for him.

Why now?

Why here?

She had lived in Colombia when he'd last seen her. Her brother Juan had hired a unit of Hunters to help defeat a group of local guerrillas. They'd gone out on a mission and he'd returned to a massacre at the compound. All of Juan's security team was dead. Juan and Selena were missing.

He'd feared the worse.

He hadn't given up, though.

All his energy had gone into finding her in Colombia. She had blocked him from sensing her thoughts and feelings. He refused to believe that her silence meant she was dead. That was too painful to even consider. He would die trying to find her, because accepting that she was gone, wasn't an option.

The night air was cool and sounds of barking dogs and night owls gnawed at the edge of his consciousness. Catal took a deep breath and blocked out everything. He focused on her. Fear and anxiety flooded him. She was in trouble, and she was in the house that he was headed for.

He was lightheaded with relief.

There was still time to help her.

He spotted a hand signal to his right. Partlan was motioning for him to climb the fence. He nodded and edged along the shrub covered border. He pushed away the white berries of the firethorn bush and was rewarded with torn skin. He shook his hand and continued through the barrier. All that mattered was that she was beyond the wall. She needed him, and he wasn't going to fail her.

The fence was stone, with an electric wire running along the top. Malac was at the house's junction box on the street dealing with the perimeter alarms and security. Catal took a deep breath and tried to mind connect with her, but still she blocked him. He shook free of his regret. He had to focus on the job at hand. Later, he would make things right with her.

"It is safe."

Malac's voice reverberated in his head. He jumped up and hung onto the first handhold protruding from the wall. The stones were warm from the retained heat of the day's sunlight. It was a welcomed contrast to the brisk breeze of night. He clenched his arm muscles and pulled his body up, reaching for the upper ledge with his free hand. His feet dangled in the air before he heaved himself to the top. Two strands of coiled wire ran along the edge. It pricked his skin, but no electricity flowed through. He nodded to Partlan before jumping to the damp grass below.

He was inside the estate's grounds.

Firbin joined him next, followed by Ranon, and Partlan. Breanon stayed on top of the stone fence as lookout. His body was angled along the edge, his rifle and scope scanning the house and gardens. He would remain there until it was safe. Malac would manipulate the security and communications from outside the compound. Once his job was finished, he would follow the others into the house.

They grouped together at the base of the fence. Partlan took the lead. Catal veered to the right and kept pace. He'd done similar operations for many years. There was nothing complicated about it, but it didn't pay to be preoccupied. Just knowing she was near was distraction enough for him.

Partlan put his hand up for them to wait.

Memories came flooding back. Hot and humid nights spent in the jungle wrapped in each other's arms. Kisses that lingered. Tongues that dueled. Sighs as their bodies twisted against each other, teasing and exciting with each movement. Catal's body hardened just thinking about the love they had shared.

The slam of a door brought him back to the present.

His ears strained as he made out the echo of feet on concrete. He was hiding in the dense garden foliage a few yards away from a fountain. The steady splatter of water from its spout was interrupted for a few seconds. Someone had stopped for a cooling splash of water. Catal held his breath and waited for the sound of receding footsteps.

The darkness surrounded him, along with the seclusion and luxury of the estate they had infiltrated. The call for help had come from here. It had been verified before Ardal, their leader, had sent them on the mission. Everything looked normal, but it was a façade.

Two children had been abducted.

Partlan motioned them forward. Catal kept his body low to the ground, his powerful leg muscles straining as he crept closer to the house. The whole south side of the building was glass. Bright lights shone from the inside, but there was no movement. It was too exposed. Only those who wanted to be seen, would occupy these rooms.

Catal couldn't blame them.

Fame had its price, and the first one was privacy.

The entranceway to the estate had been ten deep with paparazzi. Iron gates twenty feet high and controlled by electronics kept even the most determined photographer at bay. The only way to get access had been from the forested area to the south. They had skirted through the neighboring estates to reach this one. So far they'd been undetected, but now the real problems began. Police and FBI were stationed around the house.

That was good. It might mean that there would be leads to follow. Catal had some experience with kidnappings. He'd been involved in a few investigations when he had hired out as a mercenary. The others in the unit were more familiar with recovering the victims of abduction. They would never have done anything as dishonorable as snatch a child. He'd learned a lot in the past months with Ardal's unit.

Like the others, he was from another world, Cygnus. He'd been on Earth since he was ten, but it wasn't until Ardal's unit had crashed on the planet last year, that he'd fully understood what it meant to be an elite warrior. Ardal was the commander, and he'd taken Catal into his unit and finished his training.

This was the first recovery mission he'd been deployed on. It was a common operation for Hunters on Cygnus. They followed the trail left by others, and rescued those that needed it. Catal now lived by the same Sacred Code that all Hunters vowed to obey. After this mission, he would have earned the right to be a full member of Ardal's unit. His training would be finished.

"The rear door is clear." Malac's voice whispered in his mind.

Partlan nodded at Catal.

That was his cue to move.

He sprinted to the edge of the house and skimmed along the wall. He was the expert on surveillance and monitoring equipment. Once he had located the main bank of computers, he would disable everything so the others could follow. At the door he moved his hand along the casement. A thin white wire ran along the edge. He pulled pliers from his combat jacket and took a deep breath before snipping it.

Silence.

He eased the door open and moved inside. It was empty. Leather bound books lined the walls and several red wingback chairs stood in the center. Everything was in pristine condition. A room straight out of a design magazine that was probably used for interviews and photo ops. He leaned against the wall, gun ready, and waited a minute to be certain no one was coming to investigate. He released the breath he'd been holding and then crossed the room.

Their knowledge of the house was limited. The security room had to be on the main floor and common sense would put it at the rear of the house. Catal hoped that would be enough. He didn't relish wandering around this mansion for long. He had a job to do. Once the area was secure, the rest of the team could help.

He crept down a hallway and heard the distinctive noises of pots and pans being banged together. He glanced in at the huge expanse of cupboards and gleaming stainless steel. There was a woman in a maid's uniform standing at the sink. Her back was to him, so he slid past the doorway and moved further down the hall.

The next two rooms he came upon were a laundry and a storage room. To his right, across the hall, was a closed door. Catal twisted the handle and opened it a few inches. Banks of screens and glowing lights glared back at him. A guard, with his back to him, was doing a crossword puzzle. He was seated in front of the computers. Catal pulled the taser from his side pocket.

Ardal's orders were clear.

No unnecessary casualties on this operation.

The jolts of electricity made the guard's body shake and then go limp. Within seconds, Catal had gagged and tied him to his chair. By the time the guard recovered, Catal would have finished his work at the computers.

His fingers flew across the keyboards as he rerouted the camera feed and disconnected the monitors at the rear entrance. He'd been lucky. The guard was sloppy. Otherwise, his entry to the house would have been noticed. Catal shook his head. Most humans took the easy way out. Within a couple of minutes, he had all cameras online again and had looped a feed that showed no activity. It was safe for the others now.

"Coast is clear."

"What coast?"

Catal rolled his eyes. He forgot that the others were new to English and Earth. Idioms did not work with them. They took the words too literally. He really had to start teaching these guys the nuances of the language.

"The security is off-line. You can enter now."

The guard shifted in his chair. Catal looked behind his shoulder. The guard had twisted his body so that his arms were high on his back and his chair was tipped back on two legs. Having a hostage was a new situation for him. Usually, he killed the people he encountered.

"You'll hurt yourself." Catal's voice was devoid of emotion. "Struggle is useless. We mean no harm, but this was the only way to access the house."

The guard tried to shout through his gag and he bucked his body so the seat jumped across the floor. Catal shook his head. He checked the bindings before securing the chair to a table bolted to the wall. The man might struggle, but he wasn't going anywhere. Catal pulled a syringe from one of his pockets and jabbed it into the man's upper arm. It was a sedative and should keep him quiet for a while. He left the room.

"We are in." Partlan's voice echoed in his head.

Within seconds, the rest of the team was beside him. Partlan took the lead. They crept down the hall until they reached a large foyer. A massive crystal chandelier hung in the center of the ceiling. The walls were covered in a soft green silk material and the dark marble floor was glossy enough to reflect their feet. The entry screamed elegance and money on a large scale.

Voices were coming from a room on the left. They moved along the wall and crossed in front of a staircase that wound in a curve to the second floor. A matching set of stairs was on the opposite side of the entryway.

"You can't risk it." A male's voice shouted. "It's too dangerous. The FBI has procedures in place for a reason."

"It's not your son." The words were a sob. "I want my baby home."

"We're doing the best we can Ms. Nevins." The man's voice was conciliatory. "You have to trust us. We've done this many times before."

"How many times have you been successful?" A different man's voice, husky and low, asked.

"We win more than we lose." The man's gruff answer was barely audible.

Footsteps alerted the team that someone was coming to the door. They retreated to the wall, hiding in an alcove below the staircase. The door opened and a tall, slender man exited. He was dressed in a dark suit, and after he closed the door behind him, he straightened his tie and smoothed his jacket. With a deep sigh and a shake of his head, he moved to the opposite side of the vestibule and went into a room leading off a side hall.

"Let's go."

They hurried across the foyer. Catal and Partlan stood on one side of the door while Firbin and Ranon took the other. Their guns were drawn. When everyone was in place, Partlan nodded and opened the door. He entered first. Catal and Firbin were next, with Ranon bringing up the rear.

It was a room designed for comfort. A dark brown sectional couch was situated in front of a fireplace. Above the mantle was a huge flat-screen television. There were a couple of chairs upholstered in soft beige opposite the couch. Pillows of all shapes and colors were strewn on the furniture and floor. A long, narrow table rested against the far wall, its top was covered with liquor bottles and glasses. This was the room where all pretense was dropped.

A man and a woman were the only occupants.

Their faces were well known to anyone who went to the movies or read magazines. Nikki Nevins and Steve Walker. The darling couple of Hollywood. He was dark and brooding. She was blonde haired and blue-eyed innocence. They'd been married for almost ten years with only the odd rumor of a problem. Steve stood when they entered the room.

"Who the hell are you?"

"We are here to help." Partlan's voice was low. "Someone called us."

Nikki's eyes widened as she scanned them. "Are you some kind of private security group?"

Catal smiled. She wasn't as dumb as the press made out. "You could say that. We're called in when all else has failed."

"We didn't ask for anyone's help." Steve Walters crossed his arms and flopped back on the couch. "You can leave."

Nikki held her hand up. "Not so fast darling. These men look quite capable." Again her eyes scanned them, lingering on Partlan with a slight smile.

"Size doesn't mean they can be trusted." The actor's voice was scornful.

Nikki went and sat on the edge of the couch's arm. She draped an arm over her husband's shoulders. "Somehow they managed to get inside the house. The FBI have everything monitored, not to mention our own security. They must have some talent."

Steve shrugged. "We've decided to let the police handle this."

Partlan cleared his throat. "If you did not request us, who did?"

"Me."

They all turned to the voice coming from the door. A slender female, with dark black hair pulled back into a ponytail stood there. She was no more than five feet tall, but her eyes dared anyone to come near. Catal's heart stopped for a second before starting back at a furious beat. Joy and relief leapt through his body. He thought he'd never see her again.

Selena.

The one woman he couldn't forget.

Catal took a step toward her, but stopped when she put her hand up. Her eyes widened with recognition. A flicker of desire came to life deep within their brown depths. His mouth went dry and his breath halted in his throat.

She remembered.

The color drained from her face and she shook her head in slow denial. The next instant her eyes blazed fury. Her jaw clenched and she chopped the air with her hand. Catal was thrown back by the rage and hatred in her glance. He swallowed his words of greeting. She didn't want him here.

He pushed away the agony that settled in his chest and focused on the others. There would be time to talk with Selena later.

"Why the hell would you call someone else in?" Steve sat forward on the couch, his arms dropped between his denim clad legs. "We're taking care of everything, including the ransom money."

"You're forgetting my son was also abducted."

Selena's words ripped through Catal. She had a son? That meant she had found another man. His chest tightened and his breathing stilled. He knew it was the most likely reason she'd blocked him, but it still pierced his soul. She was the only woman he would ever love. To know she had turned to another was the worse pain he had ever experienced.

"We haven't forgotten Tarrin." Nikki's voice was low and soothing. "The FBI thinks it's best if we follow their procedures."

"The boys have been gone a week." Selena crossed her arms. "Tarrin would have come back if it were possible."

"Are you suggesting that Gates can't handle himself?" Steven stood and took a step forward.

Nikki touched his arm. "Selena was only speaking about her son. We all know that Gates would escape if it were possible."

"Tarrin would never leave Gates alone." Selena walked into the room. "We need help."

"And you think these men can find the boys?" Steve shook his head.

Selena nodded. "I know they can."

"How?" Steve's tone was belligerent. "You're the nanny for Christ's sake. How would you know anything about them? They look like soldiers."

"I didn't always live in the United States." Selena's voice was defensive. "Besides, they advertise on the internet. If you have a problem, they help."

"We can't take the chance that they'll mess things up." Nikki's voice was conciliatory. "It's best to leave this to the authorities."

"We do not fail." Partlan crossed his arms. "Our help was requested and we are here."

"What do you know about kidnapping and children?" Nikki's eyes narrowed. "It looks like you'd be more comfortable in a gun battle."

"We have handled these situations many times. We are Hunters. Searching for people is what we are skilled at."

Nikki frowned. "Like bounty hunters?"

Partlan looked back at Catal with a raised eyebrow. Catal moved forward to interpret. "No. We are warriors, but part of our training is finding what is lost."

"Warriors." Steve's voice rose to a shout. "Are you kidding me?"

"They are the best." Selena's voice was firm.

"What right did you have to call in men like them?"

"The right of a mother." Selena clenched her hands into fists. "Your efforts are going nowhere. I want my son returned before it's too late."

Steve lunged toward Selena. Catal jumped in front and grabbed the man by the throat. He lifted him off the ground and shook him. Nikki screamed and rushed to defend her husband, but Partlan blocked her.

"Put him down." Partlan's voice was a low demand. "He will not harm the woman."

Catal threw the actor to the ground. He crossed his arms and blocked access to Selena. His eyes narrowed as he continued to watch Steve. The man was rubbing his neck and glaring at him with hatred. He didn't care. If all Selena wanted from him was protection, then that would be his role. She might reject him, but he would never betray her.

"By Cygnus and Warrior, I will not have any human threatening my pair bond." Catal forced his breathing to slow. "That is the code by which every Hunter lives."

Chapter 2

He was the last person she had ever expected to see again.

Her heart beat in a furious staccato as she let her eyes roam over him. Catal hadn't aged a day since she'd last seen him. Tall and broad shouldered with dark hair and eyes, he stood out in a room. He always had.

Her mouth went dry and she started to tremble as she remembered the feel of his arms around her. She still woke up in the middle of the night restless with the memories of their lovemaking. After all these years, she still craved his touch.

Then she remembered his betrayal.

Selena's body tensed and her fist clenched as she motioned for him to stay away. She lifted her chin and glared at him. How could she forget his betrayal? The love she thought they had shared had never been real. He'd only been stringing her along so he could infiltrate her brother's defenses. He'd succeeded once, but never again would she trust him.

Now he was making a claim that he was her pair bond. She didn't know what that meant, but he'd given up any rights to her eight years ago. All she needed now was for her son, Tarrin, to be found. She tried to move, but Catal blocked her.

"It is the code." The man who looked to be the leader nodded.

Selena inhaled as three of the warriors surrounded her on all sides. Catal still stood in front of her with his arms crossed. All she wanted was her son back. That's why she had contacted aHunter4Hire. The name of the organization was different from the old days in Colombia, so she thought that Catal would no longer be involved. Back then, they had just called themselves Hunters, so Selena had believed she'd be safe.

Her hands clenched into fists and she gritted her teeth together. "What do you mean pair bond?"

"You are my pair bond and we did mate." Catal's tone was gravelly and low.

His voice had always sounded like that after they'd made love. A shiver of desire curled deep in her womb. She pushed it away.

"That was before you betrayed me." Selena moved past the giants who surrounded her and turned to Nikki. "I called these men in because they're the best."

"They're mercenaries." Nikki's eyes narrowed. "Where would you have heard about them?"

"I had a life before coming to the United States."

"Can they be trusted?"

Selena shrugged. "We're out of choices. The boys are running out of time."

"We're doing everything possible." Steve picked himself up off the rug. "The FBI say the drop information should come soon."

"They've been gone for a week." Selena fought back the panic that was twisting in her gut. "There's something wrong. I feel it in my bones."

"My son was taken too." Nikki's tone was cool. "I know the FBI has everything under control."

Selena threw her hands up in the air. "This isn't a contest. Our boys are in danger."

Steve went to Nikki and put his arms around her shoulders. "That's not a reason to hire thugs."

"We are Hunters." Catal moved to her side and crossed his arms. "Our training makes us the right people to call in."

Selena battled between approval and revulsion. To be standing so close to the only man she had ever loved was torture. To know he had betrayed her was hell. He was unparalleled as a soldier. The sooner Tarrin was found, the easier life would be.

"Where did you find these guys?" Steve's voice was contemptuous. "And what is a hunter."

The man in charge stepped to her other side. "We are warriors. I am Partlan. These are Catal, Firbin, and Ranon. We have two others outside. We are well equipped to find the boys, but we need to know the details."

"You're not the police. You have no authority in this matter." Nikki tilted her head. "Why should we trust you?"

Partlan crossed his arms. "The kidnappers will be dealt with according to our code."

Steve raised an eyebrow. "What's that supposed to mean? You let them go?"

"We will kill them."

Selena inhaled a sharp breath. It was as if she were transported to the past. Instead of the jungle, the posh surroundings of a Beverly Hill's mansion surrounded her. Catal had often said those exact words. He had a code he lived by. It was what had helped him survive.

Nikki cleared her throat. "Can you promise that?"

"Yes." Partlan's voice was firm.

Steve turned to her with wide eyes. "You're not serious? We can't have these men kill someone."

"Why not." Nikki shrugged. "They didn't consider what they were doing to Gates when they took him. Our son is in the hands of monsters. Who knows what they're doing to him. He'll be scarred for life."

"Then let the law deal with it."

"So they get away on a technicality?" Nikki shook her head. "No. I want justice."

"There has to be a better way."

"This is it. They are the last resort and we can't wait any longer."

Selena's voice was low and pleading. She had to make these people understand that the only way for the boys to be returned, was with help outside of the law. Already she was sensing that Tarrin was weakening.

Catal put his hand on her arm. "We will find them."

A rush of peace and calm filled her.

For a few seconds, she surrendered to the comfort he gave. It had been a week of hell. Every waking moment had been consumed with trying to connect with Tarrin. To feel his presence surround her was what she'd relied on to get through each day. As long as she knew he was alive she could force herself to function. When her connection started to weaken, she'd contacted the Hunters.

"How did you find these men?" Steve walked to a couch and flopped into it. "I'm beginning to think we made a mistake when we chose you as Gate's nanny."

"I had contact with them when I lived in Colombia." Selena straightened her shoulders. "You can find them on the internet."

"We are for hire." Catal walked to a window and looked out.

Selena watched him from narrowed eyes. As much as she needed their help, she didn't trust him. A shiver went through her as she considered what Catal's reaction would be if he knew how much she was deceiving him. It couldn't be helped. Her son had to be found and she would do anything to make that possible.

"So what did you look under, HitMenRUs.com?"

Selena shook her head. "I knew they called themselves Hunters."

"You mentioned your past." Nikki spoke now. "Do you know these men from there?"

Selena looked at the other men in the room and shook her head. "I've only met Catal. These others are strangers to me. I know that they're the best, though."

"How can you be certain?" Nikki hesitated a second. "This is my boy's life we're talking about."

"It is my son too."

Catal turned away from the window. "Selena contacted us. We will do what is necessary to bring her son back to her. If you have no wish for our help that is fine."

"Your so called efforts might interfere with my son's safety." Nikki's voice dripped sarcasm. "I'll stop you before that happens."

"You can try, but you will not succeed." Partlan's voice was a growl. "We do not fail. It would be a mistake to interfere."

"You're just overgrown louts on steroids." Steve rolled his eyes. "You've watched too many of my action movies, and now you think you're heroes. One word from me and your butts will be thrown in jail."

Selena glanced between the two men and fought the urge to run. A cloud had descended over Partlan's face and from the corner of her eye, she could see that Catal had edged away from the window. If she didn't do something soon, they would be at each other throats. Past experience had taught her that the Hunters would win.

"Stop." Her voice cracked. "If you don't want these men helping, I understand. I want them to find my son."

"I have vowed to always protect Selena." Catal's voice was low and sincere. "That includes her son. Nothing will stop me from doing that."

Silence followed Catal's words.

Selena fought back the sense of déjà vu. Catal had said those same words in the past and she had been foolish enough to believe him. She'd been wrong. Dare she risk trusting him again? She looked at him and her stomach clenched. Determination and strength emanated from him. She looked at the other Hunters and saw the same resolve in their faces.

"You promise you'll find him." Selena looked at Partlan.

"By Cygnus and Warrior." Partlan crossed his arms. "No woman or child has ever been hurt on my watch."

Selena believed him.

"Just how long has that watch been?" Steve's voice broke the spell that Partlan's declaration had woven.

"Eighteen years." Partlan turned to the actor. "I have been fighting since the year I turned fifteen. I killed my first man when I was thirteen. My ability in battle saw me promoted to the High Council's personal guard."

Steve's mouth gaped open for a second and then he leaned forward. "That's impossible. Nobody goes to war at that age."

"A Hunter does." Partlan's voice was firm. "We are trained from birth to be the best."

Steve laughed. "You've been watching too many science fiction movies. What planet are you from anyway?"

"We are from Cygnus."

"You're good, I'll give you that." Steve shook his head. "You should be writing screenplays."

"We do not jest." Partlan turned back to Selena. "We need the details of the abduction."

"Wait." Nikki's voice was urgent. "I want you to rescue Gates too."

"What?" Steve grabbed his wife's arm. "These guys are lunatics."

"No." Nikki shook her head. "I believe them about being the best fighters. That is what we need to get our son back."

"They just told you they're from another planet." Steve's voice rose. "They're certifiable."

"We do not lie." Partlan gave Steve a look of disgust. "That is a trait only humans have. We are the best warriors in the universe."

Selena's head felt as if it was full of cotton balls. Her stomach churned with nausea as Partlan's words echoed in her head. It was obvious he didn't understand Steve's sarcasm. She glanced over at Catal and found his dark obsidian eyes boring into her. There was a flicker of emotion within their depths and something that looked like an apology. It couldn't be true. She'd made love with the man. He was definitely not an alien.

"Selena, you contacted these men. Do you trust them?" Nikki's strident voice interrupted her thoughts.

She glanced at Catal and then moved her eyes to Nikki. Did she believe them? She knew they were the best soldiers on the planet. Her brother Juan had sworn he had never seen better fighters, and Juan knew what he was talking about. He'd been fighting since he was a young man.

She had been eighteen and innocent when she'd first met Catal, but even then she knew he wasn't like other men. As the younger sister of the leader of a paramilitary group she been exposed to men her whole life. She'd warded off their passes since she'd turned sixteen. Catal was different. There was a connection. He made her feel safe and she couldn't' resist him. Her whole world had revolved around him until he had betrayed her.

She cleared her throat. "I have seen them fight. They are better than anyone else in the world."

Nikki nodded. "I've decided. I want you to find Gates also. I will hire you no matter what the price."

"There is no fee in this case." Partlan crossed his arms. "Catal has declared Selena his mate. We are sworn to protect the mates of our brothers. Her son is family now."

"But Gates isn't." Nikki's voice was soft.

Partlan glanced behind at the other two men who nodded. "The boys were taken together, so we will find them both."

Nikki heaved a sigh. "Thank you."

Partlan nodded. "Tell us where the boys were abducted from."

Before Nikki could speak, the door opened and one of the FBI agents who had invaded the house rushed in. "We've received more information."

He came to an abrupt stop when he noticed the other men in the room. His eyes bulged and he reached for his gun before shouting, "Intruders."

Firbin grabbed the agent's arm that held the gun and pushed it up. A shot fired into the ceiling before Firbin had wrestled the weapon out of his hand. He elbowed the agent in the gut. The man dropped to his knees on the rug. Firbin kneed him in the chin and sent him sprawling backwards before dragging him upright by his jacket lapels.

Racing footsteps came toward the room. Catal, Partlan, and Ranon stationed themselves at the door. Firbin dragged his opponent to the far wall.

One by one, the warriors disarmed and subdued the ten agents that rushed into the room. The men were relieved of their guns and pushed against a wall. Firbin kept a pistol trained on them. The last agent at the doorway was Special Agent Kelly. She was in charge.

She scanned the situation before entering the room with her gun drawn. She stood at least six feet tall with blond hair that was scraped back into a tight bun. Her navy blue pant suit hung loose about her body, but Selena suspected she hid her beauty behind nondescript clothes. It was probably the best way to maintain her authority over so many men.

Partlan grabbed the weapon out of her hand. Deep blue eyes flashed anger. She reached for a second gun behind her back, but Partlan clasped her arm and held his hand out for the weapon. She sighed and handed it over. He didn't let her arm go. Instead, he led her into the room and closed the door behind them.

"We mean no harm." Partlan glanced over at the other agents against the wall. "If we did, these men would be dead."

Agent Kelly gave him a long look before she nodded, and then eased her arm out of Partlan's hand. "Why are you here?"

"I called them in." Selena's voice was hesitant. "You're working hard to find Gates, but I needed someone to find Tarrin."

"We are working to save both of the boys, Ms. Duarte." There was a mild reproof in Special Agent Kelly's voice.

Selena didn't care if she had upset the FBI. Life had taught her that the rich and powerful were the only ones that got taken care of. No one was really looking for Tarrin. He was just the illegitimate son of the nanny. If the son of two famous movie stars hadn't been kidnapped, Selena doubted that there would have been any FBI agents looking into the case.

"I know these men's reputation. They'll find the boys."

"So shall we." Agent Kelly glanced at Partlan. "Let my men go."

"Do I have your word they will not attack?" Partlan crossed his arms. "I do not want to hurt them."

Agent Kelly nodded. "We'll hear you out before I decide what to do. You broke the law by breaking into here, but I'm impressed. Not many could breach our security."

"It has holes." Partlan nodded to Firbin, who started to hand the weapons back to the agents.

Agent Kelly only raised an eyebrow when Partlan gave her back her guns. She holstered them and turned to Selena. "Explain about these men. Do they have anything to do with your brother's activities?"

"What are you talking about?" Selena asked.

Agent Kelly tilted her head at Selena. "Are you going to tell them about your life in Colombia or should I?"

"What life?" Selena's breath caught in her throat.

"A life that included murder, torture, drug smuggling, and the targeted disappearances of people considered undesirable." Agent Kelly's voice became stern. "You were a member of one of the most notorious paramilitary groups in Colombia. You are well versed in kidnappings."

Chapter 3

"You think I know something about the boys' abduction?" Selena could barely get the words out.

She felt as if the floor had dropped from beneath her. She swayed, and if Catal hadn't put an arm around her shoulder, she would have fallen. She had put that life behind her. She should have guessed that nothing was forgotten, especially by government agencies. They'd probably been waiting for the right moment to pounce.

She had been a young girl and sheltered from her brother's activities. They lived in a splendid house and had every luxury. She had never thought to question where that money came from. The land had been in her family for years. Handed down from father to son for as long as they could remember. Political turmoil had never touched the Duarte family until her parents had been kidnapped and killed by guerrillas.

Her brother changed after that. No longer did she have any friends from the village. She was sent away to a private school and only when she rebelled at sixteen, had she been allowed to continue her education at home. That was when she realized how different her brother had become. He was surrounded by security teams and hired mercenaries. The house was an armed camp with bodyguards and guns visible everywhere. He lived in constant fear. Never had she thought that her brother's suspicions might become reality.

The day after Catal's betrayal, Selena had fled Colombia and her brother. All she wanted was to escape the violence and bloodshed. When she'd found out she was pregnant, she had vowed her baby would never grow up as she had. The United States seemed to be the safest place to raise a child. Nothing in her past had prepared her for the mind numbing horror of these past few days since Tarrin's kidnapping. She had been too young to understand when her parents had been abducted, but now she knew what Juan had lived through. She understood his fear and need for revenge.

"You can get back to your jobs." Agent Kelly motioned for the other agents to leave. She only raised an eyebrow when she saw Firbin and Ranon follow the agents out of the room.

"What kind of mother do you think I am?" Selena's voice was a hollow whisper.

"I have wondered." Agent Kelly walked further into the room. "You must admit that it is a possibility, given your background, that you would know how to orchestrate a kidnapping."

"I rejected that life and all its violence." Selena straightened her shoulders. "Tarrin is an American citizen."

"What about your brother Juan?" Agent Kelly crossed her arms over her chest. "He's never renounced his cause. In fact, he's quite a powerful man now."

Selena shrugged. "I can't tell you where my brother is, but I know he would never hurt Tarrin. He's family."

"Don't you find it strange that a woman as privileged as you, would renounce everything for the life of a nanny." Agent Kelly's voice had a hint of steel in it.

"I had to think about Tarrin." Selena moved away from Catal. "Governments and causes come and go. There is no future in fighting the inevitable."

"Very profound." Agent Kelly's voice was dry. "I imagine your brother has enemies that know where to find you?"

"My son has been kidnapped and all you can do is accuse me of causing it. Is it any wonder I called in the Hunters."

Agent Kelly's eyes widened. She glanced at Catal and Partlan. "We've been getting chatter for years about a group of mercenaries calling themselves 'Hunters'. I thought you guys were an urban myth."

"We are real," Partlan answered.

Agent Kelly turned back to Selena. "The fact that you would go to the extreme of calling in these guys has me concerned. What are you really afraid of?"

"I want my son found, nothing more."

"Not good enough." Agent Kelly's tone was emotionless. "I need answers now, or I will call in backup. No matter how good these guys think they are, I will take them down."

Agent Kelly reached into her jacket to pull out her gun. In that second, glass shattered and the whirring of air passed through the room. A crack and then the splintering of wood on the fireplace mantle. The distraction gave Partlan enough time to grab Kelly's gun. He spun her around and pulled her second weapon from her back.

"I have never broken the Sacred Code and hurt a woman." Partlan put the weapons into his combat vest. "Do not make me chose between you and Catal's mate."

"Where did that shot come from?" Hysteria was evident in Nikki's voice. "I thought you said we were safe."

"It is one of my men." Partlan pushed Agent Kelly into a chair. "I think we should continue this discussion without accusations."

"I'm doing my job." Agent Kelly tried to stand, but Partlan put a hand on her shoulder.

"Perhaps, but two children are missing."

Catal led Selena to the armchair beside the agent. She sank into it with a sigh of relief. She didn't think her legs could hold her much longer. The visions of her past life were horrible. Worse, was the thought that it might have been the reason Tarrin had been taken.

"Selena's brother would not harm the boy." Catal stood with his legs wide and arms crossed. "It is more likely that the boys were taken because of who Gates is. His parents are celebrities. Abducting their child will make the kidnappers infamous."

"You obviously don't know Juan Duarte." Agent Kelly rolled her eyes. "He has a list of crimes longer than most streets."

"It depends on which side of the government you are on." Catal's voice held a note of reason. "The man fights for his beliefs and what he thinks is best for his country. It wasn't so long ago that the United States felt the same about organizations like his. They did train and arm them in the beginning."

"We have never condoned their violence." Agent Kelly leaned forward in her chair. "They don't know what they're fighting for any longer. It's just an excuse to ensure their power."

"That may be true, but I fought beside him. I know he is not capable of hurting a child."

Selena's heart skipped a beat. Surely Catal wasn't defending her brother? Juan had insisted that Catal was a traitor, a non-believer, who had sacrificed the lives of Juan's men for money. It also sounded as if Catal was unaware of what Juan had been doing recently. She'd lost track of her brother. For all she knew he might be more ruthless and powerful than he had been in the past.

"We are wasting time. Tell us about the kidnapping." Partlan's voice was clipped. "If you do not wish to share with us, then we will begin the search on our own, but it will take longer."

"They were taken at a soccer game." Steve spoke first. He rubbed a hand over his face. "It was my fault. I was late picking them up."

"You are certain this is when they went missing?" Catal's eyes narrowed. "Could they have wandered away from the game, or taken a ride with someone else?"

"We've talked to the other parents. No one saw the boys after the game." Agent Kelly cleared her throat. "They seemed to have vanished."

"Who else was at the game?" Partlan's tone was crisp.

"The usual spectators." Steve shrugged. "No one stood out. I dropped them off and made certain they were with the coach and then I went to a meeting."

"So there was nothing unusual."

"No." Steve's voice was defensive. "I've done it many times before. Tarrin is very responsible and he usually makes certain that no one comes near Gates."

A sob escaped Selena. "Tarrin always takes care of Gates."

"Which soccer field were they at?"

"Coldwater Canyon Park off of North Beverly." Steve's voice was intense. "We've gone through this with the FBI so many times, and nothing stands out."

Partlan nodded. "Tell us what is the norm."

Steve frowned. "There were the parents of the other players."

"How many?"

"There were thirty-two children and approximately seventy spectators." Agent Kelly answered before Steve could reply. "We do not suspect the children. We did interview them, but they hadn't seen anything."

"What about the other parents and the coaches?"

"They all checked out." Agent Kelly's voice was clipped.

"Why do you not know the exact number of spectators?"

"There were several photographers there." Agent Kelly cleared her throat. "It seems the soccer team is made up of a number of celebrity children. The paparazzi follow the games on the off chance that they may get a picture."

"Leaches." Steve's voice was full of venom. "It's one thing to follow me, but Gates should be off limits. These guys have no boundaries."

"Then we use them." Partlan looked over at Catal. Selena could have sworn a secret message passed between them, because Catal nodded and left the room.

"Continue." Partlan nodded to Steve. "How late were you getting back to the children?"

"Fifteen minutes." Steve sighed. "It's happened before, but the boys are always there. Usually one of the other parents waits with them until I show up."

"So this is a known behavior." Partlan's voice carried no censor.

"I usually bring them to the games." Selena shuddered and pushed back her horror. This was the first time she'd heard that Steve was so casual about picking up the boys. "Nikki asked me to attend a meeting with Gates's teacher that afternoon."

Partlan turned to her. "How many times has this happened before?"

Selena shrugged. "Maybe four times."

"It sounds as if it were a spontaneous abduction, or else the kidnapper was very patient."

"We've already considered that." Agent Kelly's voice was patronizing. "We are trained in this type of work."

"You received a ransom note?"

"The first day." Agent Kelly heaved a sigh. "It was brief. It stated that the children were safe and that further instructions would follow."

"We called the police right away." Steve leaned forward on the couch and hung his hands between his knees. "At first I thought the boys would be home. It seemed reasonable to think that one of the other parents had given them a ride, but when they weren't here, I called the police. The note arrived later that evening."

"And now everyone knows the boys are missing."

"We went to the press immediately."

"We asked them to." Agent Kelly's voice was bored. "We needed the public's help. An alert went out. Someone had to have seen something."

"And did they?" Partlan raised an eyebrow.

Agent Kelly turned away and crossed her arms. "No."

"People must have thought what they were seeing was normal or else it happened out of view of the others."

"You can't know that." Agent Kelly's voice was strident. "Assumptions can be dangerous. We have to consider all possibilities."

"People do not lie in this kind of situation." Partlan's voice was low. "They want to help. Our job is to find the truth and work from there."

"You make it sound as if we aren't doing the same thing."

"You do not have our experience." Partlan turned back to Steve. "Was there another contact?"

Steve looked at Agent Kelly. She nodded. "We received a note from Gates yesterday."

Selena jumped up. "You didn't tell me."

"It was addressed to us." Steve shrugged. "We let the FBI handle it."

"We thought it was better not to upset you." Nikki's voice was soothing.

Selena's eyes widened. She knew Nikki well enough to recognize her actress mode, and she was definitely in it now. She was playing the caring and considerate heroine. The real Nikki was completely opposite. She was abrupt and to the point. There was a reason she hadn't been told. Her heart started to pound.

"Why?"

At that moment the door opened and Catal came in. Selena turned to him and for a second forgot the anger and pain he had caused. She reached out a hand to him. Instantly he was at her side, his hand gripping hers. A wave of calm washed over her and for a second she let herself be lost in it.

She took a deep breath and turned back to Nikki. "I knew you were hiding things from me. That's why I called in the Hunters."

Nikki gave a light laugh. "You're family Selena. We would never harm you or Tarrin."

Selena shook her head. "You've kept me in the dark about the search for the boys, even though I'm Tarrin's mother. What are you hiding?"

"We have told you what you need to know." Agent Kelly's voice was brisk. "We can't be certain that you aren't involved."

The words hung in the room for several seconds.

"You think I would kidnap my own son?" Selena swallowed back her horror and let anger replace it. "How dare you suggest such thing? Why would I do it? What would I have to gain by letting my son suffer?"

"If you're behind the plot, then most likely your son isn't suffering." Agent Kelly's voice was matter of fact. "From my experience, money is usually a good motive."

"I was at the teacher meeting." Selena spat the words out. "How could I be in two places at once?"

"We've already established that you have some serious criminal connections." Agent Kelly tapped off her arguments on the tips of her fingers. "Second you have motive, which is money. You had the means and opportunity. We don't know who you've introduced Gates to while he's been in your charge. He would trust whoever you said was safe."

"You believe I would actually do that to a child?" Selena's voice rose in hysterical fury as she turned to Nikki and Steve. "I've looked after Gates since he was a baby. He's like my own son."

Steve shrugged and looked away. "It has happened before."

"Not by me." Selena's voice shook. "My own son was taken. You have no right to blame me behind my back."

"We could hardly tell you to your face." Nikki's eyes narrowed. "No one would take Tarrin. He's the bastard child of an immigrant with no money."

"You forget my so called connections." Selena sneered. "If you know about my brother, you know he's not poor."

"We also know he is capable of kidnapping."

Selena turned to Agent Kelly. "My brother is not in the United States. I haven't spoken to him since I came here."

The FBI agent shrugged. "He associated with criminals. That is more than enough reason for us to suspect you."

"My son is still missing." Selena took a deep breath and forced her voice to become calm. She didn't trust the FBI or any government agency, but she needed their information. Once they had everything, then she would let the Hunters do their work. "What was in the message you received?"

"It was from Gates." Nikki answered. "There was no mention of Tarrin, only that Gates was alone in a dark place and he wanted to go home."

"I assume there was a ransom note attached."

Agent Kelly nodded. "They are demanding ten million dollars. They were to send more instructions today."

"Those are the instructions you came in with?"

"Yes." The agent cleared her throat. "They want more money. They will let us know about the drop spot later."

"I'm trying to put the money together." Steve's voice cracked. "How much more can they demand?"

Agent Kelly looked over at Selena and then her gaze flickered away. "This is the first time they've mentioned Tarrin. It seems they won't release him without more money."

"More?" Selena choked. "How much?"

"Another ten million."

Selena's heart dropped. There was no way she could raise that kind of money. She might be able to contact her brother, but she hadn't a clue how to go about it. Besides, she didn't want his blood money. She'd vowed to sever all connections with him, and she had. Her only hope was for Steve and Nikki to help her. She would find a way to pay them back once Tarrin was home safe.

"I don't have that kind of money."

"I can't raise anymore." Steve's voice held regret. "I'll be lucky to have enough for Gates."

Catal cleared his throat. His hand tightened around Selena's. "I will give it to you."

Chapter 4

"Where would you get that kind of money?" Steve's voice held disdain. "Rob a bank?"

"If necessary." Catal's voice was calm. "As it happens I won't have to do that."

"Mercenaries are well paid?"

"Yes."

Selena's despair filled him. He couldn't let it continue. If having the money would help her, then she could have everything he owned, but it wouldn't come to that. Catal and his brothers would find the kidnappers first.

"Selena asked us for help, and we will give it." Partlan spoke now. "If that means giving the cash for the ransom, then so be it. I doubt it will come to that, though. If we do have to exchange money for the boys, we will get it back."

"I don't want you messing up the FBI operation." Steve punctuated each word with a pointed finger at Partlan. "They have everything under control."

"It's obvious you had no intention of trying to save Selena's son." Catal's words were harsh. "There is no need for us to coordinate with you further."

"What about my son?" Nikki's voice was frantic. "You promised that you would find him also. Are you just going to abandon us because we didn't tell you everything?"

"We gave our word." Partlan's voice was devoid of emotion. "There would be no honor if we did not try and save both boys."

Catal could feel a surge of relief flow through Selena. The tension in her body eased. He wanted nothing more than to take her in his arms and reassure her that he would find Tarrin. He sensed her rejection. She still blocked him. What had been between them once, was no more. If she hadn't been in desperate need for her son, she would never have contacted aHunter4Hire, and he wouldn't have found her.

She hadn't wanted him in her life. She'd moved on with another man and had a child. She had put him behind her forever. He could accept that she didn't want to be his mate, but what caused him anguish, was that she had blocked him.

"We will need photos of the boys." Partlan spoke to Agent Kelly. "Details of the ransom request would be helpful."

"I can't give you either." Agent Kelly pushed herself up from the chair. "I haven't a clue who you are. You might be worse than the kidnappers. My superiors would have my job if I let you anywhere near the case. You already know too much."

"As you wish." Partlan turned away from the agent and focused on Nikki. "Do you have a photo?"

"Of course." Nikki moved to a chest of drawers near the window. She pulled out a large picture and handed it to Partlan. "This is his most recent school picture."

Partlan glanced down and nodded.

Partlan's commands to Catal were by mind connection. *"Go with Selena and get a photograph of her son. See if you can find out any information she didn't tell the police."*

Catal reached a hand to Selena. "We need a photo of Tarrin."

Selena hesitated a second. She refused his offered help and stood on her own. She walked to the door and Catal followed. They went down a hallway toward the rear of the house where he had first entered the premises. They passed the large kitchen and went through the laundry room. At the end of the room was a doorway that Selena opened.

It was a small apartment. A main room with kitchen facilities and a sitting area, and two smaller rooms attached. It was sparsely furnished. There was a battered wood table and four chairs that held the chipped remnants of black paint. A threadbare grey checked couch and chair, and a small flat-screen TV on the wall. It was adequate.

"How long have you lived here?"

"Since I fled Colombia." Selena went to the table and picked up a picture. "This is Tarrin."

Catal took the photo. It showed a solemn looking boy with dark hair and dark eyes. He frowned. If he hadn't known better, he could have sworn the boy looked like a young Hunter. That was impossible. Hunters did not have children.

"How old was he here?"

"He had just turned seven." There was a catch in Selena's voice. "I had saved enough money for him to have a new outfit for picture day. He got to pick it out himself. He looked so handsome that day."

"He looks big for his age."

Selena nodded. "He is. That has made it difficult at school. The teachers and other children forget he is younger than he looks. Nikki and Steve are constantly complaining about his behavior with Gates."

"Is he in trouble a lot?"

"No." Selena's lower lip trembled. "He is strong and sometimes forgets that when they wrestle together."

"You said he watches over Gates." Catal looked up from the photo. "Shouldn't that be the other way around?"

"You would think so, but no." Selena sighed and sat in a chair. "Gates is a fragile boy. The best thing his parents did was hire me to be his nanny. I swear he spends more time in our tiny apartment than he does in the rest of the house."

"You love both of the boys."

"Yes." Selena looked up at him, her eyes full of fear. "I know Nikki and Steve don't think of Tarrin in the same way. They only care about saving Gates."

"You didn't have to be in trouble to contact me." Catal put the picture in his combat vest pocket. "I have looked for you for years, but you blocked me at every turn. Even when I couldn't sense you any longer, I continued to search."

"I had to put you out of my life." Selena's voice became strident. "After what you did to the others, I couldn't bear the sight of you."

"What I did?" Catal frowned. "I don't understand."

There was a knock at the door. Catal motioned Selena to stay seated, and then he opened the door a crack. It was Firbin. He threw the door wide and let the man come in.

"Partlan is having a problem with the celebrities." Firbin gave him a crooked smile. "Is it always this way with humans?"

"Only the rich and powerful." Catal shut the door. "Where is Ranon?"

"He is tapping into the FBI surveillance. He will join us soon."

"Selena, this is Firbin. He is an expert in explosives." Catal pulled out the picture of Tarrin. "This is the boy we are searching for."

Firbin took the picture and studied it for several seconds. He looked up at Catal with a raised eyebrow. "He is only seven?"

"He's big for his age."

Firbin nodded. "He is dark like a Hunter. That will make it easier for us to remember him."

Another knock at the door, and then Ranon entered. "We should leave."

"What about the paparazzi outside?" Catal took the picture of Tarrin and handed it to Ranon.

"The FBI were thorough." Ranon looked down and then handed the photo back. "We will start with their information from the paparazzi."

"How can they possibly help?" Selena sounded exasperated. "You're wasting time going over the ground that the FBI already looked at."

"We never waste time." Ranon's voice was low. "Our methods may be different, but they are effective. You asked for our help. Do you still want it?"

Catal could see the emotions that crossed Selena's face. She had never been able to hide anything. There was fear, anger, doubt, and resignation. In the end she nodded, her shoulders sagging a bit.

"I trust you."

"Good." Ranon went to the door. "Partlan wants us out of here."

Catal and Firbin followed, but Selena's voice stopped them. "You're not going anywhere without me. I'm coming. This is my son and I'm tired of being left in the dark."

Ranon looked at him. "*She is your mate. You decide.*"

The answer was easy. He wanted Selena next to him at all times. It might not be the best thing for the investigation, but knowing where she was would keep him focused on doing the job that needed to be done. He needed her near, but his need for her to be safe was greater. The only solution was for him to stay with her.

"It's too dangerous." Catal crossed his arms. "I'll stay here with you."

"No." Selena's voice was firm. "I don't want you."

Catal pushed away the stabbing pain that pierced his heart. Her words were a death sentence in their finality. He turned to Firbin. "Will you stay?"

"Of course." Firbin walked over to the couch and sat. "I will make certain she is safe."

"Good." Catal turned to Ranon. "Firbin can keep an eye on the developments here. That way we'll be able to keep pace with the FBI."

Ranon nodded. "Let's go."

Catal looked back at Selena. She had her arms crossed tight as if she were trying to hold herself in place. He longed to gather her close and reassure her that everything would be alright, but she looked fragile enough to break. He wouldn't do that to her. She was a proud woman.

"I will let you know the minute we have news."

Selena nodded. "Thank you."

"*I am always here for you.*" Catal whispered the words to her through his mind. He wasn't certain if she heard or not, but her shoulders seemed to relax. He nodded and then followed Ranon out of the apartment. Partlan was waiting for them in the hallway.

"We will leave through the back and then circle to the front gates." Partlan eased the rear door open. "The FBI still haven't found how we entered."

"The guy in the monitor room should be awake soon. Then all hell will break out." Catal's voice was grim.

The men raced in a crouched position until they reached the fence. Breanon was still in position, his rifle trained on the house. He lowered his weapon when they had climbed the fence. They made their escape without any noise. When they had circled back to the front, Malac joined them. Malac had completed his surveillance on the paparazzi, and photographed each of them. They went back to their van.

Ranon handed Catal a computer memory stick. "This is the FBI information I copied."

Catal raised an eyebrow. "They didn't see you?"

"Firbin distracted them." Ranon grinned. "The boy is learning more than just explosives. He thrives on this planet."

"I'm glad someone does." Catal's voice was dry. He loaded the stick on the computer and then took the camera Malac had used, to download the paparazzi faces. His fingers flew across the keys. He hacked into one of the secure police sites and ran the photos through their data base.

"It should only take a few seconds to start bringing up addresses."

"What system are you using?" Malac leaned over his shoulder.

"I'm trying the local police first." Catal watched the screen as pictures flew by. "They'll probably have most of these photographers on record due to previous run-ins with the stars. These guys aren't selling pictures if they don't create a bit of conflict. If that doesn't work, then I'll look into their driver's licenses."

One by one the pictures settled on the screen with addresses attached. Catal downloaded the information onto their portable units. Then he opened the FBI documents. With the other men leaning over his shoulder, they scanned the information. It was a pretty detailed list of the things the FBI had already done. There was one thing missing.

"There is no mention of paparazzi at the soccer field." Partlan leaned away from the computer. "Steve Walters said everything was normal."

"Normal for that man means photographers." Catal nodded. "Some of these guys outside the house may have been there."

"They will have pictures." Partlan moved to the front of the van. "We'll divide up and start searching their houses and computers."

"We need to get the ransom money also." Catal's voice was brisk. "Chances are we'll find the boys before it is needed, but we should be prepared."

"I've informed Ardal." Partlan sat in the passenger seat. "Lorcan told him that there is a large enough stash in the Los Angeles area. We'll take care of that after we visit the photographers."

Catal heaved a sigh. Lorcan had been the leader of his unit of Hunters before they had joined with Ardal. He had a network of safe houses and emergency monies stockpiled across the country. This was one of those times when Lorcan's instinct for survival was a benefit.

Breanon started the van.

They pulled away from the curb and started down the road.

Catal was empty inside. He had left a part of himself behind with Selena. Her words before he left were confusing and made him feel as if he were missing an important fact. He shook off the sensation. He needed to focus all of his attention on finding the boys. After their work was done, he would figure out why Selena had cut him out of her life.

"Catal." Partlan's voice jerked him back to the present. "You and I are together. Breanon will stay with the vehicle, and Malac and Ranon will team up. Before we start, you need to explain about your pair bond.

Catal sighed. He knew that his fellow Hunters would be curious. He had never mentioned having a mate before. What was the point when she had blocked him from her life years earlier? It wasn't until he'd seen Ardal with his mate Fiona that he'd realized he had bonded to Selena.

"I didn't believe in pair bonds until Ardal mated." Catal's hands balled into fists. "I knew that I had a connection with Selena. We had met when I was leading a mercenary unit in Colombia eight years ago."

"So you bonded." Partlan shook his head. "Why deny it?"

"I wasn't certain what it was. Lorcan had insisted that we not get close to the people we worked for." Catal threw his head back. "None of us had ever been tempted by human women before. Being with Selena meant I was guilty of betraying everything that we stood for. I was not only attracted to a human, but deeply connected on a level I didn't understand."

"So you bonded and mated?"

"Yes." Catal's body shook with the remembrance of the mating. "We spent three months together. It was heaven."

Partlan cleared his throat. "What happened?"

"We went out on a mission and when I came back she was gone." Catal pushed back his pain. "There had been an ambush at the compound. Her brother's security team was massacred. She was not among the dead, though."

"Surely you knew whether she was alive?" Ranon's voice held disbelief. "You left without finding her?"

"When I went on the mission, I still sensed her. Afterwards, nothing. It was as if she were dead, but I knew that wasn't the case. If she had died, I would have died also. The connection was that strong."

"What did you do?"

"I searched for weeks, but I couldn't find any information. Eventually I had to return to my unit, but every opportunity I got, I went back and searched for her."

"A Hunter does not usually fail when he searches." Partlan's voice was skeptical.

"I didn't have the years of training that you've had." Catal gave a weak laugh. "Only now do I know how limited I was in my searching. I never considered that she would have left her country."

"What will you do?" Ranon gave Catal a sympathetic look. "Is there any way we can help?"

"She still blocks me. Her fear for her son has meant she has dropped some of her guard." Catal looked out the window. The streetlights reflected back at him. Misery filled his soul. "The pain of being mated and then rejected was more than I could live with at times."

"How did she know to contact us about the boys?"

"Her brother was the leader of a paramilitary group. He hired us through Lorcan originally. We always referred to ourselves as Hunters." Catal turned back to face the others. "All these years of silence and she knew how to contact me."

Partlan nodded. "You have carried your pain alone. Now you have us to share it with. We will do whatever we can to ensure that your mate's son is returned to her. Perhaps then she will listen to you."

"She doesn't even know that I'm not from Earth." Catal cleared his throat. "I didn't trust humans enough to be honest with her."

"When the time is right, you will tell her."

They drove in silence until Breanon stopped the van on South Alameda Street in South Los Angeles. Malac and Ranon got out.

"Our search is a block away on East 42 Street." Partlan gave the instructions in a clipped voice. "We will meet you there when you've finished."

Breanon drove another block, and Partlan and Catal exited the van. The houses on the street were small with large iron fences and gates across the front yards. It was easy enough to find the one they were looking for and climb the fence. Breaking into the bungalow was a simple matter of jimmying the lock with a small slotted screwdriver.

The stale odor of garbage and dirt assailed them when they entered the side door. The floor was littered with take-out restaurant boxes and dirty clothes. The main room had a torn leather couch and a huge table with computer monitors and keyboards set up. Partlan rifled through a stack of photos while Catal attacked the computers.

He found a file with the date of the abduction and opened it.

Success

Pictures of a soccer field with young boys running around, filled the monitor. "This guy was there."

Partlan threw the photos aside and looked at the display. He pointed at one picture. "Magnify that one."

The image of Steve Walters and two boys running behind him filled the screen. Catal moved to the next one. Steve was talking to one of the other parents and the boys were moving away. He continued to scroll through the pictures. They documented all of Steve's actions, but none of the boys after they started to play. When Steve left, the pictures changed to another celebrity.

"There's nothing there." Catal tamped down his frustration.

"It is a start. Copy the files so we can look at them more closely in the van."

They met up with Ranon and Malac at the van. They'd had no luck at all. They continued on in the same way through the night. They tracked down all of the paparazzi's residences and checked their computers and photos. In total, they visited thirty residences. Only two other photographers had been at the soccer field the day the boys were abducted. They copied their pictures and when they were finished investigating, they loaded all of the images onto their computers in the van.

Catal went through each of the pictures several times. He scanned the photos with the boys in them first. Next, he looked at the spectators. He made note of all those who were on the field that day and compared it to the FBI list. After a third run of the photos, he stopped at one that had bothered him from the first. He had to enlarge it several times to spot what was out of place in the picture.

It showed Steve Walters arriving with the boys. Behind him, almost lost in the trees were two men. They had their cameras raised to their faces, but their clothes and posture were recognizable. They were two well-known paparazzi; brothers who worked together most of the time. They always dressed in camouflage overcoats no matter what the temperature or weather. They were large men and looked like lumpy balls because they overfilled their pockets with camera equipment.

The brothers weren't on the FBI's list of people at the park that day.

"Did we find anything at Mike and Nathan Gordon's house?"

Malac leaned toward Catal. "They were home. We decided to try again later."

Catal nodded. He continued to scan the photos, stopping at one that showed the boys near the two photographers. They seemed to be talking together. In the next set of pictures, they were gone.

"The Gordon brothers were at the park that afternoon, but the FBI doesn't mention them."

"Then we need to see the pictures they took."

"It goes deeper than seeing their pictures." Catal pointed to the photo of the men talking to the boys. "I think they might be our kidnappers."

Chapter 5

Selena paced her small living room. Dawn was breaking on the horizon and she'd spent another restless night. Her stomach churned and she popped another antacid. Sleep was impossible. When she closed her eyes, she had visions of Tarrin crying for help. Every possible scenario replayed itself in her mind like an endless loop of a horror film. Exhaustion left her brain full of cotton balls and made her question every decision. She'd been right to ask for help from aHunter4Hire.

Details of the kidnapping had been kept from her. She'd left Colombia because she wanted to be free of the lying, cheating, and killing. Learning to survive on her own in a strange country had been difficult, but it had been honest. Now she knew differently.

She thought Nikki was a friend and there was a bond of trust between them. To find out that Nikki thought she was capable of kidnapping Gates cut deep. Almost as deep as Catal's betrayal. His treachery had cut to her soul.

How come his presence gave her comfort?

She should have forgotten him years ago, but Catal was the only man she had ever desired. He was part of her essence, as necessary to her as breathing. It was a truth that hid deep within her. She wasn't prepared to admit that to anyone, least of all herself.

Selena straightened her shoulders and pushed Catal out of her mind. He was unworthy of her love. She had made a life for herself without him. She had a fantastic job and a wonderful son. That was the way she wanted it to stay. The only thing she needed from Catal was his help in getting Tarrin back.

Why did she feel so empty?

Seeing him was as if the past years hadn't happened. She longed to throw herself into Catal's arms and let him take care of everything. It was just a throwback to when she had been young and trusted in true love. She wasn't that person anymore. Catal's betrayal had forced her to grow up. That and finding out she was pregnant a month after arriving in the United States.

There was a sharp knock at her door and then it opened. Steve Walters came in and slammed the door behind him. The dishes in her cupboard rattled and Selena backed up a step.

"How dare you bring criminals into my home?" Steve's hair was disheveled and he looked as if he'd spent a sleepless night too.

Selena's heart raced at the thunderous expression on his face. "I asked for help."

"From known criminals and mercenaries?" Steve's nostril's flared. "Why didn't you just ask one of the gangs from south LA for help? You would have got a better response."

Out of the corner of her eye she saw Firbin stand. "These guys will find the boys."

"The FBI have it under control." Steve took a step toward her. "I want to know how long you planned on hiding your background from us."

"My past life has nothing to do with the kidnapping." Selena took a deep breath. "I left that behind years ago."

"Don't you think it was something you should have told Nikki before you accepted the job?"

Selena held Steve's gaze. "Nikki knew that I had a past I was running away from when she hired me."

Steve shook his head. "I told her at the time that she couldn't just pick a nanny up off the street, but she defended you."

"I've done nothing wrong."

"What about this criminal brother of yours?" Steve's voice rose. "The FBI seem to think he might be involved."

"Juan doesn't know where I am." Selena fought back the pain of leaving her brother. He had been more of a father to her until his need for vengeance had taken control of him. "I haven't spoken to him in years."

"But you know where he is."

Selena shrugged. "I've heard rumors. Believe me, he's not involved in this."

"Why should I trust you?" Steve leaned close. "You put on this goody act, but all the time you're nothing but a piece of trash that Nikki picked up on the street. Just having you in the house has put Gates life at risk. I should kill you for that."

Firbin reacted with a speed that took Selena's breath away. She'd forgotten how quickly a Hunter could move. Firbin held Steve against the wall by the throat.

"I will kill you for disrespecting a woman."

Steve struggled, clawing at Firbin's fingers.

Firbin tightened his hold.

Selena grabbed Firbin's arm. "Put him down. He is angry. Steve would never hurt a fly."

Firbin looked over at her. "You are Catal's pair bond. I will protect you with my life."

Selena swallowed the lump in her throat. Would Firbin still protect her if he knew how she felt about Catal? She doubted it.

"Put him down."

Firbin released Steve. He fell to the floor in a slump. He glared up at her as he rubbed his neck.

"These men are beasts."

"We are warriors." Firbin took a step back. "We do not allow women to be disrespected. It goes against the code we live by."

"So you just kill anyone who violates your code?" Steve's voice was sarcastic as he stood.

"Yes." Firbin crossed his arms. "If you wish to speak to Selena, then do so in a civil voice."

"She put my son at risk by being in my house." Steve pushed away from the wall. "Isn't there a rule about that in your code?"

"She did not harm your son."

"She knows people who could."

"That's unfair," Selena protested. "My son was taken too. All I want is for them both to be found. You know I love Gates too."

"Then you should never have accepted Nikki's offer to be his nanny." Steve rubbed his throat.

Selena shook her head. "I've been a good nanny to him."

"You pretended." Steve went to the door. "Just like you faked being such a good person, insisting you didn't want a man in your life. That was all for show."

"You mean because I refused your advances?" Selena's voice was low. "Nikki is my friend. How could you even think I would sleep with you?"

"The offer no longer stands." Steve sneered. "I wouldn't touch you now that I know your background."

"I didn't ask." A shiver of revulsion skittered across Selena's back. "You should be with your wife, not harassing me."

"You just better be certain you're not the reason Gates was taken." Steve opened the door. "I'll have the courts throw you so deep into jail that you'll never see the light of day."

Steve slammed the door shut behind him. Selena blinked back her tears and rubbed her arms. How could he even suspect her of being a part of the kidnapping?

"The man has no honor." Firbin's deep voice spoke from beside her. "How did you come to live in such a house?"

"I had no job and a baby on the way." Selena sighed and sat. "When I ran into Nikki at the park, it was heaven sent."

"Nikki hired you as a nanny right away?"

"She had a big acting job and a new baby." Selena shrugged. "She was desperate."

Firbin nodded. "This is how humans find work."

Selena frowned. "Not usually. We talked for a couple of hours. I loved Gates on sight and I had nowhere to go. She offered me a job and a home."

"You have been here many years. They do not treat you right." Firbin's voice was stern. "There is no trust or honor."

"I had nothing to do with the kidnapping. I would never hurt Gates or my son." Selena fought back her tears. "I just want the boys found."

"You are wasting energy." Firbin's voice was firm. "Catal and the others are dealing with it now."

"I can't rest until Tarrin is back with me." Selena's voice cracked. What did this man know about her fears?

"We will find the boys." Firbin nodded. "Catal is very familiar with the ways of your world. He will find them."

Selena frowned at Firbin's choice of words. "You mean he knows about Hollywood and the stars?"

"I mean Earth. You are his pair bond. You know how difficult Catal's life on this world has been. It has made him strong." Firbin grinned. "He is very good at getting information and working outside of your laws. He has helped us since the beginning."

Selena's breath caught in her throat. How long had Catal been with these men? They looked like the other Hunters who'd been in Catal's unit in Colombia, but they didn't sound the same.

"By beginning I take it that means when you met. When was that?"

"About eight months ago." Firbin's voice turned serious. "We were destined for execution and instead, our leader, Ardal ordered us to fight. We killed our captors."

It figured that these guys would get caught sooner or later. You couldn't go through life as a hired soldier and not upset some government along the way. Selena shivered with remembered fear. She'd always worried about the life of danger Catal lived.

"And Catal found you?" Selena hoped he hadn't help with the killings, but she knew that wasn't likely. Death followed mercenaries.

Firbin shook his head. "Not right away. He and his unit found us after we crashed on your planet."

"An airplane crash?"

Firbin grinned. "No."

"I see. So Catal helped you?" Selena forced her voice to stay calm. Firbin couldn't be serious about crashing on Earth. They'd talked earlier about being from another planet, but that was a joke. It had to be a misunderstanding. Even if Firbin thought he wasn't from Earth, she knew Catal was human. She'd made love to the man, and aside from being very large, he was human.

"He was one of the older Hunters who saved us." Firbin walked into the small kitchenette. "Coffee? It is one of the great pleasure of this planet."

Selena shook her head. "How did Catal help you?"

"They rescued our leader from the government agents who wanted to kill him. After that, Catal stayed with us, helping us create new identities and lives. He is very knowledgeable."

"Why would he do that?" Selena couldn't keep the confusion from her voice. This didn't sound like the man her brother claimed deceived them. Juan had insisted that someone had made a higher offer for Catal's services. He had betrayed Juan and slaughtered everyone.

Firbin's eyes widened. "Hunters help each other."

"So you just announced that you were part of his organization and they accepted that?" Selena frowned. "There had to be some other reason."

"He is one of the brotherhood. Even though he crashed landed on this planet when he was ten, he is still one of us." Firbin turned back to the coffeemaker. "His training was interrupted, but he learned many excellent skills surviving on Earth."

Selena's legs felt weak. She sat on a nearby chair and put her arms on the table. "So Catal is from the same place as you. That means you knew him before you came here."

"No. He is clan Saidir and older than me."

"Did you all grow up in the same town?" Selena's head started to spin and she gripped the edge of the table to stay upright.

"All Hunters are trained on Beligia which is an outer moon of Cygnus."

"And that place isn't on Earth." Selena forced back her hysteria.

Firbin swung around. His eyes scanned over her face. "You did not know." It was a statement, not a question.

"He forgot to mention that detail."

"He said you were his pair bond." Firbin sat beside her and took her hands in his. "I assumed you would know this about him."

Selena shook her head. "He never told me anything about himself or his true mission when he was fighting in Colombia. He pretended to be working with us, but all along he was our enemy."

"I do not know what his assignment was." Firbin's eyes narrowed. "I do know he would not do anything dishonorable."

"How can you be certain?" Selena's voice was low. "You didn't know him then."

"He may have been a mercenary, but he still had honor. He would not have been disloyal to those who hired him."

"What if the people who really hired him were a government agency that wanted to destroy my brother and other paramilitary groups?"

Firbin looked at her for several seconds and then shrugged. "This is something you need to ask him. Catal acts with honor now and I know he would never betray his pair bond. No Hunter would."

At that moment Selena heard a buzzing noise. It seemed to be coming from Firbin. He reached up and hit what looked like a mini blue-tooth communicator on his ear. He frowned and then hit it again.

"The FBI have news." He stood and walked to the door. "You can stay or come with me."

"It's about my son." Selena pushed the chair away. "I want to know what is happening."

Firbin moved to the front of the house, but kept Selena behind him. When they reached the room where Nikki and Steve were, there was a cluster of agents already there. Firbin let Selena move to the front of the crowd, but he kept her within arm's reach.

Agent Kelly was speaking. "They have decided on a ransom drop. They've set it up for this afternoon."

"That's not enough time to get that amount of money together." Steve's voice was frantic. "The bank just told me that they couldn't help."

Agent Kelly held out her hands in a conciliatory manner. "We told them that when they called, so they've decided to lower the ransom back to ten million dollars."

Firbin grunted.

Agent Kelly turned to him with narrowed eyes. "Do you have something to say?"

"They do not sound like very experienced kidnappers if they cannot decide how much money they want. Are you certain they have the boys?"

"We've asked to speak to the boys, but they've refused."

"That is not a good sign."

Nikki gasped. "You don't think Gates is alive."

Firbin crossed his arms. "It is possible."

The world started to spin. Selena felt her legs give way and she would have fallen if Firbin hadn't put his arm around her. He eased her into a chair. Until now, she had refused to believe that something horrible might happen.

"Tarrin is alive. I still feel him with me." Her voice was weak, but Firbin heard her.

"We need to make certain before the ransom is given."

Agent Kelly cleared her voice. "This is not our first kidnapping. We have asked for a proof of life and they have agreed. So you both can stop thinking the worse. Once we have the proof, then we will agree to the drop."

"What is the proof?" Firbin asked.

"We need a picture of the boys with today's newspaper." Agent Kelly's voice was stern. "They will be sending that to us shortly."

"How will it be delivered?"

"They'll email it to the FBI."

Firbin nodded. "We will need time to get the drop site ready."

"You're not invited." Agent Kelly turned away from Firbin, but before she could speak the door of the living room opened.

Catal and Partlan walked in.

"I told you to leave." Agent Kelly clenched her fists. "This is an FBI investigation."

"The FBI are waiting for proof of life." Selena's voice was faint. "They've given them a ransom demand."

"I'm not telling you where the exchange is taking place." Agent Kelly's eyes narrowed as she turned to Selena. "You are to have no further contact with these men. I don't want them finding out anything else."

"We don't need your information. The drop site is at Greystone Park." Partlan's voice echoed through the room. "We already have two men stationed there."

Chapter 6

"How the hell do you know that?" Agent Kelly's raised voice reverberated through the room.

Partlan crossed his arms. "I told you that we are determined. We broke into your system hours ago."

Agent Kelly's eyes narrowed. "I'll have you arrested."

"You could try." Partlan turned to Nikki and Steve. "Do you have the money?"

"No." Steve's shoulders slumped. "It's Saturday and the bank is closed. Besides, that kind of cash is difficult to get together. We might look as if we've got plenty, but we spend it. It takes a lot of money to keep up to Hollywood standards. I still need a bit of time to raise all of it."

Selena sagged against the back of her chair. "We've known for a week. I thought you'd made arrangements to have the money on standby."

Catal moved to her. He clasped her hand in his and squeezed. "We'll make certain the money is there. There will be no excuse for the boys not to be exchanged."

"How do you plan to do that?" Steve's voice was belligerent. "I've been trying to raise the cash for a week."

"We have our share now." Partlan's voice was cold. "We do not waste time on such trivialities when the lives of children are involved."

"You're lying." Steve stabbed his finger at Partlan. "No one can raise that kind of cash in a few hours."

Partlan motioned behind him and Breanon walked in with a black sports bag in his hands. He passed the bag to Partlan, who threw it at the feet of Agent Kelly. She bent and opened the bag. Bundles of green bills came into view.

"You can count it. There is the ten million that we promised."

The tight grip on Selena's chest loosened. She took a deep breath and looked at Catal. He was looking down at her with unblinking eyes. A surge of calm and tranquility flowed through her. She fought back tears of relief. She heaved a sigh and turned back to the others.

Agent Kelly zipped the bag shut and stood. "This doesn't mean that you can come to the drop site. We'll have the area covered. I won't stand for your interference."

"We brought the ransom money." Partlan raised an eyebrow. "We deserve to hear the details."

"I'm in charge here." Agent Kelly shook her head. "I'll have you guys locked up. By the time you get out, we'll have the boys back home."

Partlan crossed his arms. "It would be easier if you stopped wasting time and let us help."

Agent Kelly frowned. She seemed to consider it for a few seconds and then shook her head. "No. Bakker get these men out of here."

Catal released her hand. "I'll contact you when we have more information."

Serenity eased through her. She knew that the Hunters wouldn't leave it to the FBI. That's why she'd contacted them in the first place. They would use whatever means possible to be at the drop site.

Partlan shrugged off Bakker's hand and left the room, followed by the other three Hunters. There was a tense silence once they were gone. Nikki gave her an accusatory look before turning her attention back to the FBI.

"What is the plan?" Nikki's voice was matter of fact. "I assume that you will leave the money once we know that Gates is alive."

Selena's stomach sank.

"The money was given by the men I hired." Selena forced her voice to stay firm. "I need to know that Tarrin is alive too."

"Of course." Nikki waved aside her objections. "We want both of the boys alive."

Agent Kelly looked at Nikki. "We will do everything we can, but I have to warn you that these exchanges are not always straight forward."

"What do you mean?" Selena's voice caught in her throat. "Are you saying the boys won't be given back?"

Agent Kelly raised her hands in a conciliatory motion. "I'm saying that the drop may happen first, and the boys returned later. Our goal is to follow whoever picks up the money. They should lead us to the boys."

"What if they don't go to the boys or you lose track of the kidnappers?" Selena's voice was a whisper. She fought down nausea and straightened her shoulders.

"Then we wait until they keep their part of the bargain."

Silence followed Agent Kelly's words.

"Is that the best plan you have?" Nikki's eyes were narrowed. "Wait and see?"

"We could have done that ourselves." Steve crossed his arms. "We risked Gates' life just by calling in the FBI."

"You were right to call us, Mr. Walters." Agent Kelly lifted her chin. "We've done this many times. You have to trust us. The best chance you have of getting the boys back safely, is with us."

Agent Kelly turned on her heels and left the room. The rest of her agents followed. There was an eerie silence after the FBI left. Agent Kelly's words hadn't inspired hope. The authorities had their procedures to follow, but surely they had a better plan for getting the boys back.

Selena cleared her throat. "Now you know why I called in outside help."

"Let's just hope they don't mess things up." Nikki turned and walked to the fireplace. "Gates is all we have in the world. I couldn't bear to lose him."

"It's no different for me." Selena pushed back her pain. "Both of the boys have to be saved."

"It won't be because of anything you did." Steve's tone was an insult.

Selena looked at the two people she had considered friends. It was insane that they should think she had something to do with this kidnapping. She loved Gates. She'd die if anything happened to Tarrin. A wave of weariness washed over her. Suddenly, she was too tired to deal with anymore accusations.

"You called in the FBI and I didn't object or doubt your decision. Show me the same courtesy." Selena stood. "If it wasn't for the Hunters, we wouldn't even have the ransom money. We can rely on them to get the boys back alive."

"Are you suggesting I'm not reliable?" Steve jumped off the couch, his face contorted with rage. "I'm not the one with a criminal brother. I've done everything possible to get the boys back."

"You're the reason they were taken in the first place."

The words were out of Selena's mouth before she could stop them. The past week had been hell. She had tried hard not to blame Steve for leaving the children alone, but when all was said and done, he had failed. He had let his career come before the welfare of the boys.

"You bitch." Steve spat the words at her. "If Nikki hadn't taken you in where would you be today?"

"Nikki has been a true friend." Selena nodded. "This wouldn't have happened if you had picked the boys up from the soccer game on time."

"None of us are free of blame here." Nikki stood between Selena and Steve. "We all could have taken better care where the boys were concerned. Selena could have trusted us with her past, and we should have taken better precautions. Children of famous people are always targets for kidnapping."

Steve's shoulders sagged and he flopped back on the couch. "I never thought something like this could happen."

"None of us did." Nikki turned to Selena. "We know you love Gates. If we had known about your background that might have influenced the steps we took to protect the boys."

Selena's chest tightened. She recognized the look Nikki was giving her. Her beautiful face was poised in lines of remorse, but her chin was lifted high. The tone of her voice dripped regret. Selena had seen this act before. It was one that Nikki used when she was preparing to fire one of her assistants. The years of friendship counted for nothing. Once the boys were brought home, she'd be expected to pack and leave.

"I told you I was running from my past when we first met." Selena's voice was defensive. "You knew that there were things I couldn't talk about."

"True, but I thought I could trust you." Nikki shook her head. "I let you take care of my baby and gave you a home to live in. The least you could have done was be truthful."

"I was honest." Selena's voice shook. "I told you I had escaped from a horrible life in Colombia. You said you didn't want to hear about it."

Nikki shrugged. "You made it sound as if you were the victim. I was already upset enough about having to leave Gates with a nanny. If I'd known you were one of the perpetrators I would never have let you in my home."

"I'm not guilty of what the FBI is accusing me of." Selena's voice rose as she put emphasis on each word. "I never hurt anyone."

"What about Tarrin's father?" Nikki's words hung in the room for a few seconds before she continued. "You swear you were an innocent, but you lived in your brother's home. That means the only men you would have met were those that worked for him."

Selena's breath caught in her throat. "Why are you asking me this now?"

"Maybe Tarrin's father is ruthless enough to kidnap him."

"He doesn't know he has a son."

Selena's voice was low. The memory of the torment she'd gone through when she'd found herself pregnant threatened to overwhelm her. She had been alone and without a job. Nikki's offer of employment had been heaven sent. Nikki and Steve were just starting out in their careers and lived quietly. The fame and paparazzi had come later.

"Who is he?" Nikki's voice was strident. "We need to know so the FBI can investigate him."

"I suppose the FBI has already suggested him as a suspect?"

"They're very thorough." Steve spoke from the couch. "Especially when it comes to background checks. I've learned a lot from them."

"He betrayed me and I left. I found out I was pregnant after I was living here. He doesn't have any idea about Tarrin. If he did, he would be here helping to find him."

"I suppose we'll have to take your word for that." Nikki crossed her arms. "Did you have any enemies in Colombia?"

"Everyone is fighting each other." Selena sighed. "Do you really want to know about the life I lived in Colombia? I'll tell you every detail, but I can promise that neither Juan, nor Tarrin's father, had anything to do with this abduction."

Nikki bit her lip. "I don't want to listen to your horror stories. It was bad enough learning that you were involved with mercenaries and have a brother who is now a drug lord."

"We don't know that for certain." Selena shook her head. "Juan believes he is doing what is right for his country. I don't agree. That's why I left."

Nikki raised an eyebrow. "You've told us yourself that you are not the same person you were in the past. You don't know who your brother is now, or what he is capable of."

Selena sighed. "True. I still don't believe he would kidnap family."

"Well the FBI think Juan is responsible. That's why there isn't a huge concern over saving Tarrin. He's not in danger, but Gates is."

Selena's hands clenched into fists. "I sense he is in danger. I've always had an instinctive connection with Tarrin. He is afraid. That's why I called in the Hunters. You need to let them help."

Nikki looked at Steve, who shook his head. She shrugged and looked back at her. "We're going with the FBI."

A sense of defeat flooded Selena. There was no point in arguing. Nikki never changed her mind once she made a decision. She was on her own now because the FBI weren't looking for Tarrin. She had to trust that the Hunters would get her boy back alive.

"For the boys' sakes, I hope you're right." Selena turned toward the door. "I don't believe the FBI will be successful."

She left the room. All her years of happy memories had been wiped out in one week and there was nothing she could do. Nikki and Steve would never trust her again. No matter what the outcome of the abduction, she had lost her friend and her home. Hope and prayer were all that was left to her.

That and the skill of the Hunters.

Catal was waiting for her when she reached her room. He was standing with his arms crossed in the middle of her kitchenette. When she opened the door he looked up. His face was emotionless, but she sensed he wanted to speak with her.

"How did you get in?" Her voice caught in her throat.

"You know that doors and alarms don't stop me. That's why you called for our help." He leaned back against the counter. "We will not stop until the boys are safe."

"Nikki and Steve seem to think the FBI will be successful." Selena sat at the table and put her head in her hands. "I can't make them realize that they are wrong about Juan."

"Your brother was an honest man when I knew him." Catal reached to touch her shoulder, but she shifted away. "I will find your son."

His words sounded like a vow.

It was too much for Selena. The tears she had been holding at bay filled her eyes. She sniffed them back, but still they fell. A tissue was waved at her and she took it, sopping up her tears and fears. She knew that Catal would find her son. She had never doubted his skill, she just couldn't trust him enough to let him into her life again.

"The FBI are wrong about the drop." Catal's crouched down beside her. "They are missing something about this situation. No kidnappers would change their mind so quickly and easily."

"You think the boys are dead?"

Selena's heart stopped. Her stomach churned with nausea and her eyes widened as she watched Catal's face for any indication that he was going to lie to her. His eyes held hers for several seconds before he shook his head.

"You believe your son is alive. That is enough for me."

"I feel him here. His distress is mine." She put her hand over her heart. "It might sound crazy, but I know something has changed. He's afraid. That's why I contacted aHunter4Hire."

Catal opened his mouth and then shut it. He looked away and then stood. "You shouldn't have to carry this alone. I'm here for you. Don't block me."

"I had no idea you would come when I asked for help." Selena shook her head. "I have questions, but I'm exhausted. All I want is to get Tarrin back."

"I'll do what you ask." He walked to the door and opened it before turning back to her. "Trust your instincts. We will find your son."

Chapter 7

The sun was high in the sky. For June it was an abnormally hot day with the temperature already in the high eighty's. Catal blinked the sweat from his eyes and eased the kink out of his neck. The smell of fresh cut lawns and roses filled the air. He had been waiting in position since early morning. The drop was scheduled for one in the afternoon. At the rate the visitors were coming, the gardens would be full by then.

Greystone Park was located above the city off Loma Vista Drive. Built in the early twentieth century as the home for the heir to a financial empire, it had been given the name Greystone because of the amount of stone used in its construction. Now a heritage site that the city of Beverly Hills operated, it was open daily so people could stroll through its formal gardens and the mansion. The view was spectacular. The gardens immaculate. That's what made it a favorite with wedding parties. The parking and grounds were free which made it popular with visitors.

Catal had hidden himself on one of the stairways leading to the pool and change area away from the formal gardens. The brickwork was cool, but not enough to alleviate the heat of the sun. He was accustomed to hiding for hours on end. This was a minor inconvenience. What he wasn't used to was having to avoid all the park visitors and wedding guests who were making their way to the change rooms.

It seemed as if everyone decided to get married today. Catal had counted at least three wedding parties arriving for pictures. There were also guests assembling for ceremonies at the mansion, the gardens, and the courtyard. At this rate, there would be no place for the FBI to drop the ransom off that wasn't being used by wedding guests.

His chest was tight with despair. He needed to focus on getting the boys back; not happy couples. Weddings, even though it was a human custom, were a reminder of how he had failed Selena. His last conversation with her kept repeating in his head. His throat tightened and he swallowed hard to push away the pain. She didn't have faith in him. Despite everything he was doing to find her son, she still pushed him away.

Could he blame her though? He had never told her anything about himself. He'd let old fears and prejudices about humans cloud his judgement. Selena was his pair bond. She was the only woman he would ever mate with, and she didn't know he wasn't from Earth. She thought that Hunters were soldiers for hire, not an alien warrior race. Until he was honest with Selena, he had no right to expect her trust.

"Agent Kelly has arrived." Partlan's voice sounded in his mind. He was positioned opposite Catal on the path that led to the cypress walk. *"She is holding the ransom bag."*

"I've got her in my sights." Malac, who was watching the parking area from high in a basket crane, cleared his throat. *"Do the police on this planet always look so obvious?"*

Catal snorted. *"You're pretty conspicuous from your position."*

"I'm repairing the lights." Malac's voice held a note of hurt. *"I have blended in. Nobody ever looks up."*

"What are the FBI doing?" Partlan interrupted their banter.

"They're sweeping the area with a small dish receiver." Malac heaved a sigh. *"They are probably trying to pick up either our communications or the kidnappers."*

"Have they spotted you?"

"They've glanced at the truck, but moved on." Malac hesitated a second before continuing. *"They are moving down the stairs toward the formal gardens."*

"I see them." Partlan's voice was serious. *"Firbin and Breanon maintain your positions at the mansion."*

"We have the area covered. Breanon is watching the reflection pond and I am at mansion courtyard." Firbin's tone was confident. *"No one will get past us."*

Catal's eyes followed Agent Kelly as she ascended the brick stairs to the center formal garden. She had a large black briefcase in her right hand. He could hear the click of her high heels as she went up each stair. When she reached the top pathway, a large number of people came up behind her. They moved around her and then proceeded to move onto the grass. Chairs and a bridal arbor were set up at the end of the garden, near a fountain. Agent Kelly straightened her shoulders and turned right.

She walked along the edge of the lawn, skirting past wedding guests and park visitors until she was behind the water fountain. Catal's eyes narrowed. She moved out of his view for a second and when she reappeared the briefcase was gone.

"She's made the drop." Catal connected with the others. *"It's behind the fountain."*

"I am moving into position," Partlan answered.

Catal watched as Partlan turned and eased his way up the stairs from the Cypress trees to the formal garden. He wore a grey golf shirt and dark sunglasses. He moved with the stealth of a tiger along the opposite side from Agent Kelly. She was almost at the center staircase that led down to the parking area before she stopped. Her eyes narrowed and then she was talking into her earpiece.

"She's spotted you."

Catal inched away from the terrace where he had been lounging. If the FBI went after Partlan, then the plan was for him to take his place. They needed to keep the money within sight at all cost. Following whoever picked up the ransom was necessary to finding the boys. He had just put his foot on the first stair, when a commotion broke out from the center walkway. Catal pushed back into his vantage point against the wall.

"What's happening?" His voice was curt.

"A mob of photographers have swarmed the parking lot," Malac reported. *"They are moving toward the garden area."*

Catal glanced around the brick wall just as a huge crowd of paparazzi surrounded Agent Kelly. She tried to push her way free from them, but they only moved in tighter. Other agents came to help her, but they had even less success. The crowd moved onto the grass and into the wedding area.

Partlan continued to move to the rear of the garden.

"Can you see the briefcase?" Catal forced his voice to remain calm.

Before Partlan could answer the crowd of paparazzi trampled the chairs that had been set up for the wedding. They were like a stampede of buffalo, moving relentlessly toward the fountain and surrounding it before they stopped. Everything fell in the crush of their movement; chairs, pedestals, podium, and bridal arbor. It was a disaster.

Catal lost sight of the fountain.

"I am moving in." Partlan's voice was loud in his head. *"They have surrounded the entire fountain and I cannot see the briefcase."*

An FBI agent ran up the stairs from the parking area with a bullhorn. He raised it and bellowed. "If you don't disperse you will all be under arrest."

At that moment the crowd turned to him. They plunged back along the lawn in his direction, surrounding and taking him along with them. Cameras were raised in all directions. The only sound that could be heard above the raised voices was the endless clicking of camera shutters. Catal ducked back around the terrace wall. The last thing he wanted was to be captured in a picture.

"The briefcase is gone." Partlan's voice was clipped. *"Malac keep an eye on the people leaving the parking area. Firbin and Breanon make certain no one gets by you."*

"We have this whole area covered from the ground and up in the air. Ranon has the video feed going to the surveillance van. Everything is being taped." Malac's tone was harsh. *"If they are on the grounds, then we have them."*

"There are too many FBI agents in the parking area to get through there." Catal could see the mob that still surrounded Agent Kelly.

"We will search the rest of the estate by foot." Partlan's voice was determined.

That meant the paths that led through the cypress trees and to the mansion needed to be combed. Catal eased around the brick wall hiding him. He glanced at Partlan who nodded back at him. He stepped away from his cover and hurried to the opposite side of the garden. He met up with Partlan and they raced down the stairs and pathway that led away from the formal garden to the mansion.

Speed was of essence.

Visitors blocked their way. They pushed past them until they came to the front of the mansion. No one was carrying a briefcase. They stopped at the terrace that looked out over the front entranceway and drive to the mansion. It was empty.

No quarry could have gotten away so fast.

"Where did they go?" Catal's voice was low as he looked at Partlan.

"It had to be one of the paparazzi."

"Did anyone come your way, Firbin?" Partlan's voice was clipped.

"No."

"Breanon?"

"A couple holding hands, but no briefcases." Breanon's voice was dry.

"Then we need to take a second look at the photographer's residences."

"*I agree.*" Catal turned back toward the mansion and came face to face with Agent Bakker.

"Agent Kelly wants to talk to you." Bakker moved his suit coat aside to show his gun. "Now."

Partlan shrugged. "We have done nothing wrong."

"She'll be the judge of that."

Bakker pushed Partlan down the stone path. Catal followed. The FBI might think that they were in control, but it was obvious that they'd been outsmarted. Catal pressed back his own frustration at the debacle that the ransom drop had become. He'd made a promise to Selena and the last thing he wanted was to return to her without her son.

When they reached the parking lot, Agent Kelly stepped out of a large black cube truck. Her mouth was rigid and she was clenching her hands.

"I told you to stay away."

"It is a free country." Partlan tilted his head. "At least that was what I was told."

"We did nothing wrong." Catal didn't bother keeping the exasperation out of his voice. "You're the ones that botched the operation."

"We did no such thing." Agent Kelly grabbed Partlan's arm and turned him to face the van. She frisked him for weapons, taking away a pistol and knife. "You and your men spooked the kidnappers."

"Is that why the ransom money is gone?"

"How do you know that?"

"I am not blind." Partlan leaned close to the woman. "You put the briefcase behind the fountain and then you were stampeded by the paparazzi. By the time I reached the area, the case was gone."

Agent Kelly bit her lip. "How much time before they took the case."

Partlan leaned back and crossed his arms. "Are you asking for our help?"

"I'm interrogating a possible suspect." Kelly's eyes narrowed. "I can do it here, or at headquarters under lock and key."

Partlan nodded. "You do want our help."

"Just answer the question."

"They had to have taken the case when the paparazzi rushed the fountain area." Partlan's voice was serious. "That meant less than a minute."

"How do you know they didn't take it earlier?"

"Your men would have told you if they had." Partlan's eyes never left her face. "I saw no one approach the drop until it was swarmed and then it was too congested to get a clear view."

Agent Kelly's hands clenched at her side. "Did someone run past either of you?"

Catal shook his head. "I was guarding the stairs to the change rooms and pool. No one came that way."

"We checked out the other pathways to the mansion, but there were no suspicious people carrying a briefcase." Partlan frowned. "They might have ditched the case, but no one was leaving the mansion from the front entrance when we reached it."

"That leaves the parking lot and we had that covered." Agent Kelly sighed. "I want you two back at the Walter's residence for a debriefing. Where are your other men?"

"They're on another assignment." Partlan kept his voice neutral.

"Then you two can come with us."

Agent Kelly didn't give them an option. Catal was frisked by one of the other agents. He was relieved of his two guns. They didn't find the small knife he had belted to the inside of a hidden compartment in his boot. Then they were pushed into the van.

They were shoved onto a bench seat just as the vehicle start to move. Catal crossed his arms and leaned back against the metal side. He closed his eyes and listened to the orders that Partlan was relaying to the rest of the unit through mind connection. It was standard operation strategy. Malac and Firbin would review the tapes with Ranon in their surveillance van. Breanon was to follow them back to the Walter's estate and be ready if they needed help escaping custody. Once they'd determined who had taken the money they would leave the estate with or without the approval of the FBI.

Catal concentrated on remembering every detail of the ransom drop, including the people that had walked past him. No one was carrying a briefcase, or a backpack large enough to hold the ransom money. The only answer was that the kidnapper was either one of the paparazzi or had hired one of them to pick up the briefcase when they mobbed the fountain area.

They reached the house in a few minutes. When they entered, Nikki, Steve and Selena were all waiting at the door. Catal's chest tightened at the look of hope on Selena's face. She glanced behind him, searching for her son, then looked up at him. He shook his head.

Her pain was a physical stab to his gut. He almost doubled over at the intense agony that ripped through his body. He forced back his nausea and pulled Selena into his arms. He held her tight.

"We'll find him." His whispered assurance only made her shiver more violently. "I promise, I will do everything in my power to bring him back to you."

Selena let him hold her for a few seconds before her back stiffened and she pushed away. "What happened?"

"The area was swarmed with photographers." Agent Kelly's voice was businesslike. "Someone must have tipped off the paparazzi that there was going to be a ransom drop-off. Did any of you speak to the press?"

"Are you nuts?" Steve's voice was scornful. "They're the last people we'd talk to."

Agent Kelly nodded. "Alright. Who else did you tell about the drop? Nothing is ever a secret for long in this town."

"No one." Nikki's voice was choked with tears. "This is our son's life we're talking about. Do you honestly think we would jeopardize it?"

Agent Kelly shrugged. "I don't know at this point. We have to reassess our options and move forward from here. The kidnappers have their money. They should be in contact with us about an exchange for the children."

"Do you think that's possible?" Nikki's voice held a note of hope.

"It's what we agreed to." Agent Kelly pushed Partlan ahead of her into the room where the FBI had set up their surveillance. "Meanwhile, these gentlemen need to answer some questions."

Catal was grabbed by one of the other agents. He released Selena. She watched him move away with eyes that begged for answers. He sent her a wave of love. It was the only answer he had at this moment. Once the FBI were finished with their questions, hopefully the other Hunters would have narrowed down the search of the photographers who had shown up at the Greystone.

Catal was pushed into a chair.

Partlan sat beside him.

"How the hell did you get there before us?"

"We told you our men were already in place." Catal crossed his arms. "We're not the kidnappers. We're trying to help."

"You've been obstructing justice" Agent Kelly paced in front of them. "I want to know where your other men are."

"They have their orders."

"I want them here." Kelly leaned close to Partlan. "If they don't show up willingly, I will issue a warrant for their arrest."

"You have already threatened us with that." Partlan's jaw tightened. "Why not ask us your questions. You are wasting valuable time. Time that the boys have very little of."

Partlan's words seemed to force Agent Kelly back to the present. "Alright. When did you start your surveillance of the area?"

"We went there as soon as the drop was arranged."

"There's no way you could have gotten there before us." Kelly crossed her arms. "Enough lies. I want the truth."

Partlan sat up in his chair. "We were there early enough to see your surveillance van arrive this morning."

Agent Kelly stepped back. "Alright, so you made us."

"So did the kidnappers." Catal's voice was harsh. "There was no chance they were going to let themselves be caught at the drop area. You should be focusing your attention on the paparazzi that circled you."

"We've already looked at that angle." The agent stood back with arms crossed. "Did you notify them of the drop so that we wouldn't be able to follow what was happening?"

"No." Partlan's voice was curt.

"How did they find out?"

"I imagine the kidnappers told them." Catal bit back his anger. Answering these questions was wasting time. An idiot could have figured out how the press had found out and the FBI were not idiots.

"Perhaps," Agent Kelly agreed. "I still think that you and your men are holding something back."

Partlan stood. "We have told you all we know. Now we need to get to work to find those boys."

"You two aren't going anywhere."

At that moment, the telephone rang.

Everyone froze.

The sound reverberated through the still room. It rang a second time before Agent Kelly motioned for one of the agents to pick up. He grabbed the phone and listened for several seconds before motioning for a pen. He wrote with furious strokes and then hung the phone up.

"That was the kidnappers." The agent swallowed. "They were unhappy about us being at the drop site, but said that they would still honor the bargain. They want to arrange for the exchange of the boys."

The room went quiet.

Catal exhaled a short breath, forcing his heart rate to slow.

Agent Kelly turned to him and Partlan. "Do you know anything about this?"

"I have already told you that we do not have the boys." Partlan's eyes narrowed. "You do not seem to hear."

Agent Kelly glared at Partlan for a second and then turned to Catal. "What about you?"

"I am here to help my mate." Catal's voice was low. "She needs my support."

"Mate? What are you, a Neanderthal?" Agent Kelly snorted. "So Selena is your girlfriend. That means you're probably part of this plot."

"Selena is my mate." Catal straightened his shoulders. "Her son Tarrin is missing and she asked for help. I have told you this before. You refuse to listen."

Agent Kelly shook her head and turned back to Agent Bakker. "Arrange the exchange. These two are to stay here. The last thing I need is for another leak."

Partlan looked at Catal. *"I have warned the others,"* he said through mind connect. *"You should go to your mate. She will need you."*

Catal's jaw clenched. *"You don't think the boys are alive."*

Chapter 8

Selena glanced up at the clock.

Thirty seconds had passed since the last time she checked.

She bit her lip and clenched her hands tighter. She was in the front room with Nikki and Steve who refused to look at her. There was a ringing in her ears and it hurt every time she took a breath. It seemed as if hours had passed since the FBI had told them to stay put. The kidnappers had their money. Now they needed the boys back. She unclenched her hands and looked up at the clock.

Ten more seconds had passed.

She glanced away and straightened her back in the chair. Nikki and Steve had already found her guilty of taking the boys, and nothing she said could convince them otherwise. The silence in the room was deafening. To them, she was the enemy. She choked back a sob and turned away. This wasn't the time for tears.

She had to focus on Tarrin.

She loved him above all else.

As much as Nikki and Steve blamed her, they were the reason for Tarrin's abduction. She was certain of it. Her son was in danger now because she had taken a job with the Walters. They were high profile celebrities. The danger of someone stalking them, or invading their privacy was always present. She had just never considered that it might endanger her son's life. Only a maniac would hurt a child.

A door slammed shut.

Selena moved forward in her seat.

The sound of footsteps approached outside the door. She turned in time to see Agent Kelly enter the room. Agents Bakker and Smythe were pushing Catal in front of them. Her heart raced at the sight of him. She blocked the sensation. Every cell in her body longed to have him hold her close. She needed his touch now, but she had to guard her heart. Once Tarrin was found, Catal would be gone from her life again.

Agent Kelly went to the center of the room.

Catal walked over to Selena and stood beside her. She glanced at the other agents. There was no expression on their faces. Selena's stomach dropped as she prepared for the worse. She reached up and gripped Catal's hand. Strength flowed into her. She straightened her shoulders and faced Agent Kelly.

"I won't waste your time." The FBI agent's voice was strident. "We've heard from the kidnappers. They've arranged for us to exchange the boys."

A gasp of shock ripped through Selena's lungs. There was hope. She looked up at Catal and smiled, but he was expressionless. She frowned. The boys would be home safe soon. Surely this was good news?

"What?" Her voice was a raw whisper.

"The kidnappers said nothing about the boys being alive."

"Why else would they arrange for us to pick them up?" Selena's voice faded as she realized what Catal was concerned about. She shook her head. "He's alive. I know it. I sense him still."

Catal frowned. "How do you sense him?"

"Even before he was born, I had a connection with Tarrin." Selena's hand shook as she pulled away from Catal. "He's my son. I know he's alive."

"Then we will continue our search." Catal crossed his arms. "Partlan and the others will find the boys. My assignment is to stay with you."

Agent Kelly pointed at Selena. "You are not to leave. Once we have the boys, we will contact you. Nikki and Steve can come with us in the police van."

"No." Catal's voice was firm. "She has as much right as they do. We will accompany you."

The agent glared at Catal for several seconds before looking away. "You will be in a separate van and under constant surveillance."

Selena stood. "My son has been taken also."

"As you so conveniently keep reminding us." Agent Kelly turned back to Steve and Nikki. "Do you wish to come with us?"

Nikki looked at Steve and then back to Agent Kelly. "I will come. Steve will stay here and try and distract the paparazzi so they don't follow us."

"Good plan." Agent Kelly nodded. "We don't need a repeat of this afternoon."

It took several minutes to arrange the vehicles that would transport them. Selena's stomach was in a knot and her knees weak. Catal kept close to her, his presence gave her the power to continue.

Soon she would have Tarrin in her arms. Once again she would see his beloved dark eyes and grave smile, and know that everything was alright.

She refused to consider any other possibility.

Her son was alive.

They climbed into a black van along with Agent Bakker. There was another agent who drove, while Bakker stayed in the rear with Catal and Selena. Nikki went in a separate van with Agent Kelly and Smythe. No matter what the outcome of the exchange, Agent Kelly had made it quite clear that she didn't trust Selena. Selena would worry about the FBI's allegations later. Right now, she only cared about getting her son back alive.

Catal sat beside her, his back straight and unmoving. She reached out and clasped his hand. He looked down at her, a muscle in his jaw tightened, but his eyes softened. A longing to share the connection she had once had with him rushed through her. She wanted to turn back the clock and be the young girl who had believed in love everlasting. With a sigh, she released his hand and looked out the window.

The drive to the exchange location seemed to take hours. They turned down a number of streets that led into the city of Los Angeles. Slowly the houses changed from luxurious mansions to smaller well-kept bungalows and two storey homes. When they passed a group of conical towers, she knew they were in Watts.

"Is this the right spot?" Selena's voice was hesitant. "I thought this was a neighborhood where gangs arranged drugs deals, not kidnappings."

"We're following the instructions we were given."

They pulled up in front of a small bungalow. It stood out from the rest of the houses on the street because of its state of disrepair. The paint on the siding was peeling off and some of the windows were boarded up. An old van in the driveway was the only indication that someone lived at the place. She moved forward in her seat when Agent Bakker opened the side door of the vehicle and jumped to the road.

"You stay here." He slammed the door shut.

Catal reached past her, released the handle and pushed the door open. "I'm going in. I've let the other Hunters know the location."

Selena frowned. He wasn't wearing a wireless ear set. How had he told them? Perhaps they were following. There was comfort in knowing that reinforcements were coming, but it wasn't enough. She had to see for herself.

Selena slid off the seat and out of the van. "I'm coming with you."

Catal hesitated for a second and then nodded. He pulled her behind him, blocking her view. When she tried to move around him, he stopped her with his arm.

"Stay behind me." Catal's voice was low. "That is the only way I can protect you."

"The boys need to see friendly faces, not policemen." Selena gripped his shirt. "My safety doesn't matter."

Catal turned to face her. He leaned in close enough so that his words could only be heard by her. "I lived through the hell of not knowing what happened to you. I won't put your life at risk now that I've found you."

"No one is going to hurt me." Selena's voice faltered at the look of pain in Catal's dark eyes.

"If anything happened to you, I would die."

Selena's breath caught in her throat at the sincerity in Catal's voice. "I promise to be careful."

"Once I know it's safe, you can look." Catal took a step forward. "I'll try to get us closer."

Selena peeked around his back. There were police everywhere, most of them in protective vests that said FBI. She shuddered at what the boys would think about the show of force. Nikki was standing close to Agent Kelly. The two of them were leaning against the hood of the van they had arrived in. Catal took a step to the side and she followed.

"They've broken the door in." His voice rumbled through his chest.

Selena leaned closer to him, taking comfort in the shelter he provided. Her body was shivering with anticipation. A second later, a loud gun blast ripped through the air. It was followed by a second one. She moved to go around Catal. Before she could take a step, he grabbed her close.

"Wait." He stroked her hair. "The police know enough not to hurt the boys."

"How can you be certain?" Selena's voice cracked with a sob. "What if the kidnappers decided to kill the boys at the last minute?"

"That would make no sense." Catal put his hands against her cheeks and looked down into her eyes. "You said you could feel him with you. You would be the first to know if something had happened."

Selena gulped back her panic and focused. Tarrin's presence was still there with her. It was faint, though. "He's alive."

The FBI came out of the house leading a large man in front of them. He was bald, with a torn tee shirt and black sweatpants. Dried food clung to a grey streaked, dark beard that reached his chest. His arms were behind his back and he was yelling.

"You've no right to barge into a man's home." He twisted his body in the agent's hold. "I've done nothing wrong."

"We have it on good authority that you are holding two boys here." Agent Kelly stepped in front of the man. "Where are they?"

"You're crazy lady." The man's eyes bulged wide. "I know nothing about kids. I hate them."

"Then that would explain why you kidnapped them." Agent Kelly's voice was neutral. "Tell us where they are and it will go easier for you."

"I ain't saying nothing without a lawyer." The man's chin jutted out. "I'll sue you for the damage to my house too."

Another agent came out the side door. He shook his head. Selena's heart stopped for a second. Did that mean the boys were dead? She started to run toward the house, but Catal's strong arms held her close. Warmth and comfort flowed through her.

"Remember, you know he is still alive." His words where a whisper against her ear. "Chances are the boys were never here."

She looked up at him. "Why?"

"Nothing about this kidnapping has made any sense." Catal kept his voice low. "Partlan and the others are investigating another suspect."

"Do you know who did it?"

"We have our suspicions."

"Have you told the FBI?"

"No." Catal's finger pushed a strand of hair behind her ear. "They don't want our help. We have only one goal and that is to get the boys back. They want to make an arrest."

Selena nodded. "That's why I called you. I knew you would do whatever it took to bring them home."

"We won't rest until they are safe."

Tears pricked Selena's eyes. "I remember how determined you could be in the past."

"I would never hurt you." Catal's hand smoothed against her cheek. "We are bonded."

Selena turned her head away. He might not hurt her now, but what of the betrayal and pain he'd caused in the past? She couldn't forget what her brother had said. Right now all that mattered was that he save her son. Whatever it took; she didn't care.

"You still don't trust me." Catal's voice shook. "Whatever you think I've done, you're wrong. I've searched for you. All I care about is your safety and the return of your son."

"Too much has happened." Selena's voice was hesitant.

Catal sounded sincere. She sensed more than saw his pain whenever he looked at her. He had done everything she asked without question. He believed her. What more proof did she want that she could trust him? Her head ached and her stomach felt heavy. She would worry about this later.

Selena turned away and watched with unseeing eyes as the FBI agents left the house. They were carrying boxes and papers, but nowhere was there anything the boys might have used. No clothes, no toys.

"Take me home."

Catal led her back into the van and together they waited in silence until Agent Bakker jumped into the front seat. The drive back to the Walter's residence was quick. Selena held herself together, willing the pain away before it overcame her. How had a once happy and safe life become this?

At the house, she shook Catal's arm away. "I need to be alone."

She walked to her own quarters holding her body straight and tense. She was close to breaking and she didn't want anyone, least of all the man she had once loved, to see her cry. She was a strong woman, but there were limits.

She flicked on the light and locked the door to her quarters before stumbling to the couch. Tears blinded her. She sat and dropped her head into her hands. She knew Tarrin was alive, but where did they search now? Her chest tightened with agony.

"Don't tell me you've given up little one?"

Her head shot up.

Her brother Juan stood in her kitchen.

Chapter 9

Eight years had passed since she'd last seen him, but he looked the same. He was a tall and handsome man, ten years her senior. Their parents had died when she was eight, so he'd become more of a father to her than a brother. She had rejected the life he led, but he was still her brother. A surge of love raced through her veins.

"What are you doing here?" Selena wiped away her tears.

"I heard about the kidnapping of my nephew." Juan took a sip from the mug he was holding in his hands. "You did not think a little thing like a border would keep me away."

"How did you know where to find me?"

"I have always known where you were." Juan's tone was indulgent. "You are my baby sister. You might have run away from Colombia, but you can never lose your family."

Warmth flowed through her. "You weren't angry about my leaving?"

"It pained me that you felt a need to go without my knowledge." Juan shook his head. "I know I was strict, but your safety depended upon it."

"I understand that now." Selena nodded. "When I was younger, I thought you were overprotective."

"The massacre at the compound should have taught you differently if nothing else." Juan's voice dipped low. "Every day, I thank God that you were in town."

A shudder shook Selena as she remembered the horror she had returned home to. "The FBI are all over the place. It's amazing you got past them."

"They are careless. You all left in vans and only one agent remained." Juan shrugged. "It was easy to enter undetected."

"The police think you were responsible." Selena straightened her shoulders. "You can't stay here. It's not safe."

"Why would I kidnap my own flesh and blood?" Juan snorted. "It is good to see police everywhere are imbeciles."

"They think you're running drugs and the cartel has something to do with it."

"My men know better." Juan put his mug on the table and walked over to her. "I would never endanger my family."

"What have you been doing then?"

"I work the ranch." Juan gave her a crooked smile. "I am good at it. I have expanded our land and resources. I maintain a security force, though. Perhaps that is why the authorities are suspicious."

Selena sighed. "I knew you were innocent. Unfortunately, the FBI think I arranged the kidnapping with you. That's why they've kept me in the dark."

"Stupid." Juan sat down beside her. "You would never hurt Tarrin."

"My background makes me look suspicious." Selena clasped her brother's hand.

"You could not hurt a fly." Juan gave her a reassuring squeeze. "You hated carrying a gun even for protection."

Selena shuddered. "I left the fighting to you."

Juan raised her hand and kissed it. "You were a saint compared to me."

"No." Selena shook her head. "I was frightened and a coward. The only time I felt safe was when Catal and the other mercenaries joined us."

"You do not still think about him." Juan's tone was incredulous. "He has been out of your life for years."

Selena bit her lip. "I called the Hunters in to help. Catal was one of them."

Juan threw her hand down. "How could you trust them?"

"I had no choice." Selena's voice begged him to understand. "The FBI cut me out. They considered me a suspect and wouldn't tell me anything. I needed someone to get Tarrin back."

"Has Catal succeeded?"

Selena shook her head. "They are working on a lead. Catal says they should know something soon."

"They think they are better than the FBI and all the government resources at their disposal?" Juan leaned back on the couch. "Maybe they are. They were the best soldiers I ever fought with."

"Catal put up the ransom money." Selena's voice was quiet.

"You mean the rich movie stars couldn't come up with the cash?" Juan's voice held disgust.

"They needed more time." Selena kept her voice neutral.

"They had a week." Juan grasped her chin and turned her to face him. "You should have come to me for help."

"I couldn't risk it." Selena held her brother's gaze. "The FBI would have been happy to arrest you. Besides, I wasn't certain you'd want to hear from me after all these years."

"The authorities would have had to catch me first." Juan released her chin. "I'm here now. As long as you were safe, I did not interfere in your life. You always have a home with me. It is your heritage too."

"You are the oldest son. The ranch and land are yours."

"Our parents left it to both of us." Juan heaved a sigh. "They died too young to worry about inheritances."

Selena rubbed her arms. "It must have been hard when they were killed and you were left with me. You were too young for the responsibility."

"You were the same age when you got pregnant." Juan's voice was emotionless. "I did not do a good job of parenting, though."

"You did your best." Selena grinned. "I was stubborn and always knew best."

"Are you telling me that has changed?"

"No." Selena shook her head. "That's why I'm insisting you go home. It's not safe for you here."

"I'm not leaving until my nephew is found." Juan clasped his hands together behind his head. "Where were you just now?"

"The kidnappers had called to tell us that they were exchanging the boys." Selena heaved a sigh. "It was a hoax. There were no boys at the house. All the FBI did was anger a man eating his supper."

"Are you certain this man is innocent?"

Selena nodded. "Catal believes someone else is responsible."

Juan frowned. "His instincts were always good. Does he know about Tarrin?"

"No." Selena turned to her brother. "I'm torn about telling him the truth. Ever since the massacre at the compound and Catal's betrayal, I have been afraid to trust anyone."

"That was a harsh lesson." Juan's voice hardened. "One we both learned from."

"You lost all your men." Selena's voice sounded small to her own ears. "What did you do afterwards? Did you continue with the paramilitaries?"

"What was the point?" Juan's tone was bitter. "You think you are making progress, but someone is pulling your strings. You're a puppet for them, and when they're done, they kill you."

Selena shuddered as she remembered the horror of what had happened to her brother. He had almost lost his life along with his men. It had been one of the rare occasions when she'd left the ranch for a day of shopping in the city. Her bodyguard, Pablo, had driven with her and they'd returned in the late afternoon. Catal and the men in his unit went out early in the day and they weren't supposed to be back until late, or the next day.

She'd only been gone a few hours. When she'd returned her whole world had been destroyed. There had been blood and death all around her. Her brother, who had barely survived, had been helpless to prevent it. He'd remembered what he'd seen though.

"Are you certain it was Catal?"

It was a question she had asked over and over. Her brother's description of what had happened did not sound like something Catal would do. The man who had held her close and loved her to distraction, could not have committed the atrocities at the compound. That's what made it so difficult to accept.

"The man was a Hunter." Juan clenched his jaw. "He said that his government had ordered us dead. When I begged for a reason, all he would say is that he followed orders. After that, he shot everyone at the camp. If Carlos hadn't pushed me down and protected me with his body, I would have been dead too."

"But you didn't see Catal shoot anyone."

"I saw a Hunter. He told me his name was Eogan when I asked." Juan's lips flattened. "Catal and his mercenaries were working against us all the time. They took our money and then left us for dead. The only reason you are alive is because you weren't at the camp that day."

"You would be dead it I hadn't come back." Selena rubbed her brother's arm. "You were losing a lot of blood from your wound."

"There was no emotion in his eyes when he shot us." Juan's voice cracked. "We could have been figures in a video game for all that it mattered to him. My whole security force gone in the blink of an eye."

"That still doesn't prove that Catal was a part of it."

"Where were he and his men when we needed them?" Juan's voice was harsh. "The one time we could have used their special skills and they were gone. I do not believe in coincidence."

"Catal told me he was going on a mission that you had ordered."

"No." Juan shook his head. "I gave no such order."

Selena sighed. They had gone over this numerous times, and each time the result was the same. Catal and the other Hunters had been gone from camp when the attack had happened. The fact that it was another Hunter who had slaughtered everyone, made it even more suspicious. There was only one conclusion. He had purposefully left Juan and his men unprotected.

Catal had betrayed her brother.

There was no other explanation.

"You can't stay here Juan." Selena stood. "The FBI will find you and arrest you."

"If you insist. I want you to know that I am staying in the city until this is resolved." Juan pulled a cell phone from his pocket. "I have programed the number you can reach me at. It's only good for one call. Let me know if Tarrin is safe or not."

Selena took the phone and put it in her jean's pocket. No matter what the FBI thought her brother had become, she still loved him. She wouldn't endanger his life.

"I brought some money with me." Juan pulled a brown envelop out of his jacket pocket. "When this is over you won't be able to stay here. Use this to start a new life."

Selena nodded. "I wish it could be different."

Juan hugged her close. "All I ever wanted was for you to be happy. Find a decent man and make a new life for you and Tarrin. I never wanted to see you with a mercenary like Catal."

"I loved him." Selena held back the pain. "I'll never be able to trust another man again."

"Nonsense." Juan gripped her shoulders and held her away from him. His eyes stared into hers. "You must start again. I blame myself for not seeing that you were involved with Catal until it was too late to stop it. If I had been there to take care of you, none of this would have happened."

"You can't protect someone from love. Besides, I wouldn't have Tarrin." Selena forced herself to smile. "I treasure him."

"True." Juan gave her a quick kiss on the forehead and released her.

"What about you?" Selena put a hand to her brother's cheek. "Have you married? Do you have children?"

"No and no." Juan shook his head. "I have no room in my heart for love. I see no point in attachments when those you love are ripped from you."

"You've seen too much death and loss." Selena sighed. "We both refuse to trust again."

"It is safer."

"It is also lonely."

Selena looked up into her brother's eyes. She understood only too well what he felt. After Catal's betrayal she had shunned others. Tarrin had forced her back into the world, but her heart had remained locked away. She gave him a quick kiss on the cheek.

"It is time." She hugged him tight. "I love you."

Juan stood. "I am always here for you. Whatever you need."

Selena nodded. "Be safe."

Juan nodded and then turned to the door. "Remember to call me when you have news."

The next second, he was gone.

Selena sat and flung her head back on the couch. How had he managed to get over the border? He was crazy to risk capture. It would have been better if he had sent someone else to give her the money and message. Still, it was good to see her brother.

They were both survivors.

They had just chosen a different way to deal with it.

Juan had become bitter and cynical. The betrayal and loss of his men had made him turn his back on any meaningful relationships. Instead, he had buried himself in his work. The only thing he allowed himself to care for now was her and Tarrin.

She had chosen to hide. A life of safety and seclusion in exchange for love. It hurt less, but she felt empty. If she didn't have Tarrin, she wouldn't have a reason for living. A stab of pain made her clutch her chest. What would she do if he didn't come home alive?

A knock at the door made her sit up.

"Who is it?"

"Catal."

"Go away." Selena cleared her throat. "I have no wish to see you."

"I have news about the boys."

Chapter 10

The door opened before Catal had finished speaking. He fought to hide his pain. She couldn't stand to have him near, not even for a shoulder to lean on. The only thing he could do for Selena was bring her son back. He wouldn't fail. Already they had more information than the police.

Partlan had escaped the house when he and Selena were at the rendezvous. The other Hunters had started searching through the video they had taken at the exchange site. Soon they would know who had picked up the ransom and that would lead to the kidnappers. It was only a matter of time before they found the boys.

Selena brushed her dark hair from her face. By Cygnus, she was beautiful. Every cell in his body craved to pull her close and ease her fears. He forced himself to keep his hands at his side. She was too fragile right now. Any move on his part would send her over the edge.

Selena moved aside and let him enter. She closed the door and leaned against it. "What have you found?"

"Partlan and the others have been reviewing the video tape we took of the ransom drop." Catal walked into the tiny living space.

The scent of a man's aftershave assaulted Catal.

An intruder.

He pushed Selena behind him and scanned the room for the trespasser. Nothing was out of place. Selena's fist hit his back. He shrugged it off. His focus was on protection. He'd been slack in letting her return alone to her quarters.

"Who's here?" His voice was a low snarl.

"Nobody." Selena pushed at his back. "I'm alone."

"Someone has been in this room."

Selena exhaled. "Juan just left."

Catal's eyes widened and he turned around. "Your brother?"

"That's the only Juan I know." Selena's voice was sharp. "He snuck in when we were out of the house."

"What did he want?" Catal eased his muscles.

"To make certain I was safe." Selena shrugged. "I haven't seen him since I came to the United States, but he'd heard about the kidnapping. He wanted to help."

"We will find Tarrin. Juan doesn't need to worry."

"You can go unless you have some news." Selena's voice was dismissive.

Catal clenched his jaw. "We should know soon who the kidnappers are. They will lead us to the boys."

"How soon?"

"After the videotapes have been examined."

"What happens if you come up empty like the FBI?" Selena crossed her arms.

"We have another lead we are following."

"Then why aren't you there now?" Selena's eyes narrowed. "These monsters have already tricked you once."

"It would be better for the boys if the kidnappers felt safe." Catal kept his voice even. "We want them to feel secure. We want them to make a mistake."

"You don't think they have the boys with them."

"Do you?" Catal didn't hide his exasperation. "You're from a country where kidnappings are frequent. You know what we're dealing with here."

"Yes I do." Selena spat the words at him. "That's why I'm so frantic. How many kidnappings have you been involved with?"

Catal inhaled a calming breath. "More than I care to think about. I have dealt with it from both sides."

Selena gasped. "You've abducted people?"

"It was part of the job." Catal cringed at how callous he sounded, but it was too late to make apologies for the life he had lived before joining Ardal's unit. He had survived.

"How did your kidnappings play out?" Selena's voice was a whisper. "Did you kill the people?"

"No." Catal straightened his shoulders. He wasn't proud of his past, but he had never broken the Sacred Code. "There would have been no honor in that. We did what we were paid for. In the end, our victims were always released."

"What if they identified you?"

"They knew better."

"So you used fear to keep them quiet?" Selena shook her head. "Is there honor in that?"

"Perhaps not, but it was better than not keeping our word. We said if the money was paid, then the victims would be set free. We are men of our word."

"What if they didn't pay?"

"That wasn't a problem."

Catal forced his voice to stay calm. There had been times when money wasn't the reason for the abduction. Politically motivated kidnappings were meant to remove opponents. In those cases, he'd set up the victims in a new place where they could start their lives over. If they desired, he'd make arrangements for their families to meet them. Their clients had been satisfied that their opposition was out of the picture, and his honor had been left intact.

Selena bit her lip. "Who are these possible suspects?"

"We will interview these men and see what they have to say."

Catal kept his voice neutral. He believed their initial assessment of the paparazzi was correct. The kidnappers were among them, but he didn't want to get Selena's hope up if it didn't pan out. Secrecy was best at this point. The last thing they wanted was to frighten them into fleeing before they knew where the boys were.

"You mean you're going to interrogate and torture them." Selena shook her head. "You forget, I know how you operate."

"I never resorted to torture." Catal fought back his frustration. "I'm with Ardal now. We do things differently."

"How different?" Selena's tone was doubtful.

"We help those who need it." Catal kept his voice low. "We right the wrongs we find. We always do things with honor."

"Why the difference?" She raised an eyebrow. "You didn't seem inclined to change in the past."

"I have learned that some humans can be trusted." Catal kept his gaze fixed on Selena.

"Somehow that doesn't comfort me." Selena hugged her arms close to her body.

"I can't change the man I was." Catal took a step closer to her. "I am bonded to you. I might not have understood that in the past, but I have never lied to you."

Selena gave him a pained look. "I don't want to talk about your lies. Right now, all I want from you, is my son back."

Catal forced back the agony her words produced. He had failed her in the past. When he should have been protecting her, he had been away on a mission. He had followed orders, but he knew differently now. Never should he have left his mate in danger. He would make it right.

The last years without Selena had been pure anguish.

He couldn't continue to live like that.

"We need to talk."

"When have we ever talked?" Selena's voice was sarcastic.

Catal winced at her words. "True, but there are things you need to know about me."

"You told me nothing about yourself. All I know is that you are a mercenary who was disloyal to my brother."

"I never betrayed you."

"Juan disagrees." Selena's voice was weary. "He said it was a Hunter who had destroyed the camp. The truth was that you were never working for us, but for another government."

"That's not what happened." Catal wiped his hand over his face and sighed. "I came back from the last mission and you were gone. There was nothing left of the base camp except bodies. I searched each one to be certain you weren't one of the dead."

"What about your life before?" Selena tilted her head. "How long have you been a mercenary?"

Something in Selena's voice forced Catal to look at her. Her eyes didn't waver from him. In their depths, he saw wariness and uncertainty. Perhaps now was the time to tell her the truth. Honesty would be the only way to prove that he had changed. It would show that he trusted her completely.

"What do you want to know?" Catal's jaw clenched.

"Firbin hinted at something that I didn't understand."

Catal reached out for Firbin with his mind. *"What did you tell Selena?"*

"I thought you had told your mate the truth about how you arrived on this planet." Firbin's voice was apologetic. *"Once I realized she did not know, I stopped."*

Selena was looking at him. Her eyes were expectant. She stood in the center of the room, with arms crossed and shoulders back. She wouldn't settle for less than the truth. He must open himself to her and trust. She deserved to know who he was. All these years on Earth and never had he told a human the truth about himself. This was not an ordinary human, though.

This was his mate.

The woman he held close to his soul.

"When I was ten years old, I was on a training exercise that went wrong." Catal exhaled a deep breath.

"What kind of training operation does a ten year old go on?" Selena's voice held disbelief.

"My training started when I could walk." Catal's voice was devoid of emotion. There was nothing he could do about his past. "A Hunter spends his whole childhood training to be a warrior. That is one of the reasons we are the best."

"One of them? Does that mean that there are others?"

"Yes." Catal rubbed the back of his neck. This was more difficult than he had thought possible. He had buried the truth deep. He had no intention of ever telling anyone his background. It was the first brutal lesson he had learned on this planet. Blend in. Act human. It was safer that way.

"Hunters have been genetically modified to be the best warriors. At birth we were given implants that helped us focus and develop quicker."

"We don't have that kind of technology." Selena shook her head. "If we did, it would be illegal."

"Nevertheless, it is true."

Selena frowned. "Why would they do this?"

"It made us warriors. There is none better than a Hunter." Catal cleared his throat. "We had implants that provided us with chemicals and biologicals that made us stronger."

"Steroids?"

Catal shrugged. "I have no idea what they were. Besides the chemicals that helped us, there were implants that made certain we would only concentrate on our duty. They blocked our natural tendencies."

Selena shook her head and sat on the couch. "This is sounding complicated. Wouldn't strength be the only thing you needed help with?"

Catal shook his head. "We need complete focus to duty. Hunters are used for only one thing. We are warriors. Any other kind of life is denied us."

Selena was silent for a few seconds. "So you only had one job. You were soldiers."

"Yes." Catal inhaled a deep breath. "Our learning began as soon as we could walk. When I was ten, my unit was sent on a special training exercise. Our ship malfunctioned and we crash landed on Earth."

Selena gave him a blank stare for several seconds and then shook her head. "Firbin suggested that, but I know you're human."

"I am not from Earth."

Catal's heart raced. He watched Selena's face for the first signs of revulsion and fear. Her eyes widened and she looked away from him. She brought a shaky hand up to her mouth as if to stop herself from screaming. He braced himself for her rejection.

"How is that possible?" Her voice was a low whisper. "Where are you from?"

"I am from Cygnus." Catal unclenched his jaw. "It is an ancient culture run by the Kaladin until very recently. A civil war has meant that the Holman are now in charge."

"Is it far away?" Selena's voice shook.

Catal shrugged. "I have no knowledge of the distance. That is not my specialty. I am clan Saidir. We are soldiers."

"How could you have lived?" Selena turned to face him. "People don't survive plane crashes."

"The technology of the Kaladin is advanced. Parts of their crafts are engineered to survive interplanetary challenges and landings. Our teachers moved us into the protected area of the launching chamber before we crashed. About one hundred of us walked away alive. We lost many in the accident and more since we've been on this planet."

"How long ago did this happen?"

"Almost thirty-one years ago."

Selena's mouth dropped open. "You barely look thirty."

"We age differently on your planet." Catal's gaze didn't leave her face. "I have seen over forty years and most of it has been spent fighting."

He waited for her reaction. Her hands clenched in her lap. That lasted a few seconds before she slumped forward on the couch. Finally she sighed and looked up at him.

"How do I know this is the truth?"

Catal sat down beside her. "I am not lying. Just telling you this puts my life at risk."

"Then why say anything?"

"I need you to understand why I couldn't be honest with you before." Catal reached out and stroked her arm. "There are other things about me that you should know."

"About your life?" Selena's voice was soft.

"Yes, and why I didn't recognize or trust you when we first met."

"Explain." She leaned back on the couch.

"Our genetic modifications meant that we had a narrower focus than ordinary men. We are committed to our makers, the Kaladin. We've been programed to work together in a smooth and efficient manner, but there are side effects."

Selena frowned. "Like having a heart attack when you're young because of overuse of steroids?"

Catal shook his head. "We usually don't live that long. We are warriors bred and trained to succeed at any cost. Death is the reward we expect."

"So you only see one purpose in life, and that is to fight and die." Selena raised her eyebrows. "What about your parents? Didn't they have a say in what you did?"

"We have no parents. We are created in birthing chambers." Catal lowered his voice. "We are not like other men. Our makers used the implants to ensure that we would never find a mate."

Selena shook her head. "That's not possible. You and I both know that."

"That's because my implants stopped working."

"What agency would be involved in anything so cruel?" Selena's voice was doubtful. "Why would it be necessary?"

"The genetic modifications that were done to Hunters meant that we formed intense commitments and connections. It made us fantastically loyal warriors. We also formed powerful bonds with each other and our mates."

Catal glanced away. Since crashing on this planet, he had believed his life would be complete if only he could return to Cygnus. Instead, the only right thing in his existence was this woman beside him. Selena made him whole.

"You mentioned pair bonds before." Selena reached for his hand. "Explain what this means."

"A Hunter bonds only once." Catal clasped her hand in his. "He forms a pair bond. If she desires, she will become his mate."

"By mate, I assume you mean lover." Selena's voice was hesitant.

"Yes." Catal went down on his haunches beside her. "The linking with our mate is so strong that it means we will forgo everything else to protect her. It makes us poor soldiers. So the implants were in place to stop us from bonding."

"Are you trying to tell me that you couldn't commit because of implants?" Selena's eyes narrowed. "That's the most outrageous explanation for desertion I've ever heard."

"My implants probably stopped working after I crashed on your planet." Catal held her gaze. "Until I met you, I had never formed a pair bond."

"Why are you telling me this now?"

"I should have been honest with you when we first mated, but I didn't trust humans. I believed you were the enemy."

Selena pulled her hands away. "That's a poor excuse. Even on the planet you're from, there must be people you can and cannot trust."

"I was never permitted near anyone but my teachers and fellow Hunters." Catal sat back on the couch. "We are not meant to interact with others. We are meant to battle. That is the only thing that has occurred to us on this planet that was part of our training."

"What else happened?"

He shook off the panic that rose in his throat. It was a child's fears and he was a man now. The crash had made him that. Selena needed the truth from him. His fears wouldn't help.

"When we crashed, our teachers thought it would be possible for us to return to Cygnus. They tried to contact others on our planet, but our communication systems were destroyed." Catal swallowed back his terror of what happened next. "When they knew we were stranded here, they decided to try and find a way for us to return to Cygnus on our own. Your planet wasn't as technologically advanced, so they inserted themselves into some of your scientific communities and tried to accelerate your progress."

Selena swallowed. "What agencies?"

"Your space exploration and weapon developments."

"For which side?"

"Whichever country had a program. We weren't here to take sides."

"What did your teachers do with you?" Selena pushed back a strand of hair from her head with a shaky hand. "You had to be too young to help."

"We were." Catal heaved a sigh. "We were expendable. They left us to fend for ourselves."

"You were a child." Selena's voice held outrage.

Catal nodded. "Unfortunately, our crash didn't go undetected. Our teachers were able to escape, but not all of us were that lucky."

"What happened to you?" Selena's voice was low.

"I was captured."

Chapter 11

A shiver raced through Selena as she saw the dead calm in Catal's eyes. She remembered clearly the first time she'd seen that look. They had returned from a rendezvous outside the compound gates. He held her close, but when she looked up, he was gazing with unblinking eyes at a point just beyond the gatehouse. Before she could ask what was wrong, he'd pushed her behind him.

She'd barely had a chance to blink when Catal had pulled out his sidearm. In the next second, he'd reached for the knife in his boot and threw it. A harsh groan and the sound of someone falling was followed by two quick shots from his pistol. Running footsteps from the main house ended the assault, as the guerrillas retreated. Catal had seen her back to the house before leaving with the rest of the Hunters to pursue the intruders. Throughout the ordeal, he didn't speak and his eyes had the same focused calm.

She knew it was bad, but she had to ask.

"What happened?"

"Another Hunter and I had hidden under some debris near the crash site. We'd been ordered to stay put by one of our teachers."

"Why would you stay there?" Selena's tone was incredulous. "The crash site would be the first place searched."

"Hunters are bred to follow commands, no matter what the order, we obey."

"Did the other boys have the same instructions?"

Catal shook his head. "No. They were given different locations so that everyone was scattered. The teachers thought that if some of us were captured and found alive, the humans would stop their pursuit."

"You were used as a decoy." Selena stifled a moan. "How awful."

"It meant that the rest had a chance to escape." Catal shrugged. "It is a strategy often used with success. Capture is part of battle, and that's what we were conditioned for."

"What about protecting children or working together as a team?" Selena didn't hide her indignation. She took a deep breath to calm her anger. "What happened next?"

"I killed my first man that day." Catal's voice was devoid of emotion. "It was one of the soldiers who seized us. He had a gun aimed at my head and I didn't hesitate."

Selena winced. "So they took you away."

Catal's face went blank. "I had training in handling pain and torture, but it wasn't sufficient. I learned enough to last a lifetime by the end of my ordeal. These are things a warrior accepts."

Selena reached out a shaky hand to Catal. "You don't have to continue if you don't want to."

"You deserve the truth." Catal looked down at their joined hands. "I didn't understand about pair bonds before, but now I do. You are the only person I have ever told this to, not even my brother Hunters know what happened to me."

"You must have escaped or did they let you go?"

Selena tried to keep the tears out of her voice. Whatever happened to Catal, it must have changed him. She remembered the numerous scars that were spread across his body. A large cluster were on his chest and back. She'd always assumed they were battle wounds and he'd never told her different. Now she wondered.

"I escaped. The other Hunter with me wasn't so lucky." Catal shuddered. "I saw an opportunity and I took it. I told him I'd return with help. Once I found my brothers, we went back, but the place was deserted. He was gone."

"So you don't know what happened to him?"

Catal shook his head. "I should have waited until both of us could go."

"No." Selena grabbed Catal's hands. "If you hadn't escaped, you would have died there."

"The others said the same." Catal's voice was low. "It was decided that he must be dead. When we couldn't make contact with him, we stopped looking."

"Was he the only one taken?"

"No." Catal stood and started to pace in front of her couch. "Over the years, more than half our numbers have been killed by humans."

"You must hate us." Selena's voice was a whisper. "Is that why you left all of Juan's men dead?"

Catal frowned. "I never killed your brother's men."

"Juan saw a Hunter killing everyone at the camp." Selena clutched her hands together. "He didn't lie about what he witnessed."

"It wasn't us."

"The Hunter told him that he was working for another government and he was following orders. He started shooting. Juan barely escaped with his life, but the rest were massacred."

"We had orders from your brother that morning to do surveillance."

"He says he never gave you any commands." Selena's voice was apologetic. "I asked him numerous times about what happened, and he's very clear. You and your men deserted rather than guard the compound."

"Pablo brought the orders." Catal's voice was firm. "We were to scout General Ramirez, the guerrilla leader. Our orders were to assassinate him in retaliation for the kidnapping of your neighbor's daughter, Rosita. It took us two days to track him down."

"Pablo volunteered to drive me into town that day."

Selena's stomach sank. Pablo must have been the traitor. All these years she'd blamed Catal and he was innocent. Her eyes widened as she realize what a horrific mistake she'd made. If she had trusted her love for Catal, she would have known he couldn't have betrayed her brother.

"We returned from our mission to find a massacre at the base camp." Catal's voice was devoid of emotion. "I searched everywhere for you, but you weren't there. I didn't leave a body or stone unturned, even when I was ordered to stop."

"Juan said you were responsible."

"No." A muscle twitched in Catal's jaw. "We were mercenaries and took money from humans to kill, but we were still Hunters. We had honor."

"So you weren't working undercover for a government black ops agency?"

"Juan paid us." Catal's crossed his arms over his chest. "We did his bidding. We went to do the assassination that he ordered. Surely you heard that we succeeded."

"Juan said you betrayed him." Selena's voice was weak. "He is my brother. I believed him."

"So you ran?"

Selena nodded. "My love for you turned to hatred and bitterness."

"You thought I was your enemy. That is why you denied our connection."

"You weren't the only one I shut out of my life." Selena wiped her hand over her forehead. "I left my brother and country. I couldn't live with the violence any longer."

"You were afraid." Catal's words were a statement.

"You always made certain I was protected." Selena shook her head. "I was a coward. I should have waited for you and demanded an explanation, but I thought everything that had happened between us was a lie."

"Don't say that." Catal crouched in front of her. "I remember every second of our time together. It is the only true thing in my life."

"I thought you'd used me." Selena looked up at him. "How can you continue to aid me? If it had been me, I would have walked away the minute I realized who was seeking help."

"You almost did leave when you saw that I was one of the Hunters who answered your call." Catal smiled. "I would do anything for you. That is the nature of the pair bond."

Selena's chest felt as if a vice were tightening around it. Catal had never stopped loving or looking for her. He had never betrayed her. Her throat thickened at the thought of her own deception. She inhaled a shaky breath. She must tell him the truth.

"I have to confess something." She looked down at her hands. "You might not be able to forgive me."

"There is nothing you could do…" Catal started to speak and then stopped. He frowned and then stood. Selena swore he was listening to someone, but there was only silence in the room.

"We have a new lead." Catal reached for Selena.

"What is it?" Selena's voice shook.

"We were suspicious of some of the paparazzi already. Now the evidence confirms we were right."

Selena's dark eyes widened. Her lip quivered and her hands clenched at her side.

"You've found the boys?" Her voice was hushed.

"We have a suspect." Catal moved to the door. "I have to leave and meet up with the others."

"I'm going with you." Selena grabbed a jean jacket from the wall hook and slipped her arms into it. "This is my son you're talking about and I should be there."

Catal waited at the door. "I think it would be better if you stayed here, but I won't stop you from joining us."

Selena grabbed a large beach bag and threw in a sweater, pants, shirt, underwear, and a change of clothes for Tarrin. She ran to the bathroom and scooped up their toiletries. She picked up the cellphone and envelop of money that Juan had given her and shoved them in last.

Selena took her purse from the table. "Good. I need to be there when you find him."

"As you wish."

Catal opened the door and looked up and down the hall before heading to the rear of the house. Selena followed. They passed the kitchen and went through the rear entrance. Outside the air was cool. It was a welcomed relief from the humid, muggy day. The sun was low in the sky and dusk surrounded them. She took a deep breath and joined Catal.

"Are you certain they won't find us?" Selena's voice was a hushed whisper.

"We've altered the security cameras." Catal eased his way along the outside wall of the house. "It's running in a loop so they'll only see what we want them to see.

Catal crouched and tilted his head.

Sounds of the night creatures and water fountain were all that Selena heard.

He reached back and waved her over to him. She took a deep breath and forced her heart to beat at a normal pace. As frightened as she was, she now knew that she could trust Catal to protect her. She followed him as they ran through the gardens and across the wide expanse of manicured lawn. By the time they reached the outer fence, her chest was rising and falling at a frantic pace. She leaned against it to catch her breath. Catal waited until her breathing eased, then he pointed up at the fence.

The stone wall was the last barrier to freedom.

Catal glanced back at the house and then motioned for her to start climbing. She reached up with both arms and he lifted her at the waist. Her hands slipped a couple of times, but then she found a rock to hold onto. She pulled herself up, swung her leg over the smooth mortared top, and dropped to the other side. He followed her.

Once on the ground, Catal took her arm. They ran through the back garden of one of the neighbors that bordered the rear of Steve and Nikki's estate. When they reached the street, he stopped. She looked behind. There was no one following them and Catal nodded to Selena.

They crossed the road.

A block away they stopped beside a black van.

Catal knocked on the rear door. It was opened immediately. He grabbed Selena by the waist and helped her into the vehicle. He followed and shut the door behind him.

"Is this wise?" Partlan's voice was low.

"She insisted."

Catal motioned for Selena to sit on a bench that ran along the one side of the van. On the opposite side, a number of computer screens were set up. Malac and Ranon were sitting at the monitors.

Partlan nodded. "It is best that we move. There have already been FBI agents on the road. It will be more difficult to follow if we are traveling."

"Did they get close to the van?" Catal reached into a toolbox on the floor. "I don't want them to have a tracking device on us."

"They were not close enough, but check."

Catal pulled out a small monitor and scanned the van. Selena heard a few bleeps, but Catal ignored them.

"It's clear."

Selena released the breath she'd been holding. At least the FBI wouldn't be following them. Once they discovered that she and Catal had escaped, they would assume the worse. They'd take it as proof that she was involved in the kidnapping. She didn't want to worry about the police catching them before they found the boys.

"What have you discovered?" Catal's voice was low.

Malac turned away from his monitor. "We have numerous angles of the Greystone garden area. I've been looking at the ransom drop site in slow motion, screen by screen. There are some interesting points."

Firbin was driving the van and eased up as he came to a stop sign. He looked over his shoulder and grinned. "They were not clever enough for us."

"Who do we have?" Catal leaned close to the monitor.

Malac pointed to the screen. "It seems the brother paparazzi team were at the ransom drop."

Selena moved forward on the bench so she could see the video. Her eyes narrowed as she picked out a couple of familiar faces. It was two brothers that often followed Steve and Nikki. They were both wearing large dark jackets. It was an unusual outfit considering the day had been extremely hot.

"Are they close to the drop area?" Catal's eyes were glued to the monitor.

"Watch." Malac moved the mouse and the video sped up.

Selena watched as the figure of one of the brothers moved to the rear of a fountain.

"Stop." Catal's voice was clipped.

The shot showed one of the brothers bending down. Malac continued to let the video move frame by frame. The other paparazzi hid his movements, but there was no mistaking that he had the opportunity to take the briefcase.

Catal turned to Selena. "Do you recognize these guys?"

Selena shifted forward on the bench. "That's Mike and Nathan Gordon. They're often outside of the mansion."

"Is there any reason they would have had to take the boys?"

"None that I know of." Selena frowned. "I often talk to them. They've always been very friendly with Tarrin and Gates."

"So the boys would trust them?"

"Yes." Selena looked up at Catal. "Is there any reason they shouldn't?"

"They were at the soccer park the day the boys went missing." Partlan gave Selena a picture.

It showed Mike and Nathan Gordon at a park. There were a group of people standing on the sidelines of a soccer field with the players in the middle of action. Selena looked closer and recognized a number of familiar faces. They were the boys and parents of Tarrin's teammates.

"Where did you get this picture?" Her voice shook as she looked up at Partlan.

"It was in the photo cache of one of the other paparazzi." Partlan handed her another picture. "This was in another group."

Selena's eyes widened. "Did you guys steal these?"

"We copied them." Catal's voice was low. "You asked us to do everything possible to get the boys back. We are doing that."

Selena concentrated on the second photo. "Gates is talking to Mike."

"That is the last time we see the boys in the photos." Catal pointed at the picture. "They were close to a wooded area. It would have been easy to disappear in there."

Selena gave a slow nod. "Why would they have taken the boys though?"

"We are going to ask them." Partlan took the pictures.

"So you think they're the kidnappers?" Selena's voice cracked.

"They were at the drop site." Catal reached over and took her hand. "We have them on video disappearing behind the fountain where the money was."

"And they could easily hide it under their jackets." Selena finished in a low voice. "I've always been generous to them with tips of where Nikki was going to be. Steve only had one altercation with them, but he apologized and has given them preferential treatment since then."

"What was the argument about?" Catal leaned toward her.

"He broke Nathan's camera." Selena frowned. "It was almost five years ago. Steve apologized and replaced the camera. Ever since then, he has always treated them with respect."

"Why did he break it?"

"Nathan took a picture of Gates in the pool." Selena shrugged. "It was nothing, really, but Nathan climbed over the stone wall and perched in one of the trees. He used a telephoto lens. When Steve saw it, he went ballistic."

"He didn't want his son's picture taken." Catal leaned back.

"No." Selena remembered the incident vividly. It was the first time she'd realized what a risk she took by working for Nikki. She'd brushed it off at the time. There was no reason for Tarrin to be hurt by her job. Now she knew better.

"It's not unusual for celebrities to feel that way. They want to protect their children from the press." Selena looked up at Catal. "Did I do wrong by letting Tarrin play with Gates?"

"No." Catal's voice was soothing. "The boys are friends."

"There was just the one incident?" Partlan interrupted.

Selena nodded. "It's the only one I'm aware of."

"It hardly seems enough to make these men seek revenge." Malac peered at his computer monitor. "There is no mistaking that they left with the ransom money, though."

"So either they kidnapped the boys, or they know more about it than they should." Partlan's voice was decisive. "Drive to the Gordon's house."

Firbin put the directional lights on and turned at the next stop. Within in a few minutes, they were on the freeway.

"We will speak with Nathan and Mike." Catal sat beside Selena.

"You have no proof that they're involved." Selena touched Catal's arm.

A shiver of awareness passed through her. She inhaled a sharp breath. It was as if she was awakening after a long sleep. It had been years since she'd felt this thrill. She had buried her memories so deep that she had almost forgotten how intense and complete being with Catal felt.

"We won't hurt them." Catal's voice was steady. "They are the best lead we have. We need to ask them questions about the ransom. They knew the location of the drop site. That means they are either the kidnapers or in contact with someone who knows where the boys are hidden."

"I understand, but since leaving Colombia, I have lived a life of peace and non-violence. I've raised Tarrin the same." Selena's voice ended on a sob.

"There is no honor in violence just for the sake of violence." Partlan's voice was quiet. "As long as these men have not broken the code we live by, then we will not harm them."

"What is the code?" Selena's voice showed her confusion. Catal had not mentioned a code, only that he lived by honor.

"All Hunters live by the Sacred Code." Partlan nodded toward Catal. "Even as a child and alone, Catal understood that."

"The first rule is that no harm should come to women or children." Catal rubbed her hand. "If they had nothing to do with the abduction, then they haven't broken the code."

"What if they are the kidnappers?"

"We will kill them."

Chapter 12

Catal pushed back his disgust and anger. He was a warrior. There should be no emotion attached to following the life of a soldier. Yet a part of him wanted to rip apart the men who were responsible for causing his mate pain.

"No." Selena shook her head. "I want them left for the police."

"That won't be possible." Partlan spoke now. "If they have harmed a child once, they will do it again."

"The police will put them in jail for life." Selena's voice was firm. "They won't be able to harm anyone there."

"It does not make sense to keep them alive."

"I have seen enough violence and death in my life." Selena straightened her shoulders. "I don't want to be associated with any more. All I care about is getting Tarrin and Gates back alive."

"What if these men have hurt the boys?"

Selena's body sagged and she brushed her hand over her forehead. "I'll think about that. Right now, all I care about is getting the boys back alive. If these men were only involved in the ransom drop, then I want them left for the police."

Catal shrugged and glanced over to Partlan. He nodded. Selena was a woman, and as Hunters, they'd been trained to obey women. As much as he wanted to destroy these men for the pain they'd caused Selena, he would abide by her decision. If they did anything to harm Selena though, he would destroy them.

"As you wish."

Firbin slowed the van down. It came to a stop and the front door opened. Breanon jumped into the vehicle. They were in a small residential neighborhood in Central Los Angeles. The house was a bungalow painted lime green, with a link fence and gate across the front yard.

Partlan looked at Breanon. "Have they left the house?"

"No." Breanon turned around so that he faced the rear of the van. "They were here when I started my surveillance. There has been commotion in the house, but no one has come or gone."

"What kind of activity?"

"Packing." Breanon picked up a rifle. "They have also been burning stuff in their fire."

"They're getting rid of the evidence." Catal nodded. "We had best stop them."

"Any sign of the boys?"

Breanon shook his head. "They seem to be alone. If the boys are there, they've hidden them."

Partlan frowned. "Firbin you will stay with the vehicle. Pull up alongside the house and wait for us. It is time we had some answers from the Gordon brothers."

"What about me." Selena leaned forward. "I should be there."

"It's too dangerous." Catal placed a hand on her arm. He wasn't going to risk her life until he was certain the brothers weren't armed. "Once we have secured the place, then you can join us."

Selena held his gaze for a second and then nodded. "As long as you let me question the men too."

"As you wish."

Catal and the others left the van. Breanon took a position near the entrance. The large front window provided a clear line of fire into the house. The lights were blazing and the brothers could be seen inside. Breanon crouched down behind some shrubs that bordered the front entranceway. Once the house and brothers were secured, Breanon would change his position so that he could defend them from any intruders.

Catal pulled his pistol.

He eased his heart rate in preparation for battle.

He and Partlan crept along the house to the rear. Malac and Ranon positioned themselves at the front entrance.

"*Go.*" Partlan commanded by mind connect.

In unison, both teams broke open the doors at the same moment and rushed into the house. Catal entered the rear first. He skirted past the kitchen and moved into the front room. Malac was there ahead of him and held a gun to the head of Nathan. Ranon's knee was in Mike's back as he held him down on the floor. Partlan brought up the rear. He scanned the room and then shut the front curtains. That was Breanon's signal to watch for any intruders, including the police.

"Get these two into chairs."

Nathan laughed. "It won't help you now."

Catal's eyes narrowed. He pulled Nathan up by his neck and backed him into the wall. He held him up from the floor and tightened his grip on his neck.

"Where are the boys?"

"I don't know what you're talking about." Nathan struggled to get the words out. "You don't frighten me."

Catal threw him down on the floor.

He went to stand up, but Malac grabbed him by the arm and pushed him into a chair.

Malac stood back and held the pistol to the side of his head. "Answer the question."

Mike was already being held in a chair by Ranon.

"You're too late." Nathan grinned over at his brother. "You can do whatever you want to us, but it won't change a thing."

"What do you mean?" Selena's voice pierced the air. "What have you done with the boys?"

"I mean we got rid of them."

Catal went to Selena. "We told you to wait."

"When the curtains closed, I knew you had secured the house." Selena twisted in Catal's arms. "The back door was open. I shut it so the neighbors wouldn't think anything suspicious was happening here."

"Good." Partlan nodded toward the brothers who were being held in chairs. "It would be best if you let us interrogate them first. It is not a proper place for a woman."

Selena shook her head. Catal could feel the horror and panic that filled her body. He eased his hold on her and stroked a hand down her back. He sent her a wave of calm. They didn't know yet what the brothers meant. It was best not to jump to conclusions.

"Let us handle this."

Nathan snickered. "Nothing is going to bring those boys back now."

"You killed them?" Selena's voice was a hoarse whisper.

Her legs gave way and she sank to the floor. Catal grabbed her before she fell. His heart beat furiously as he watched all the life and hope go from her eyes. He forced himself to push aside his anguish at her pain. It wouldn't help get the answers they needed. He held her close.

"You said you still felt Tarrin alive." His whispered into her ear. "Hold onto that."

She nodded. She straightened her back and stood. She turned to Nathan. "What did Tarrin ever do to you?"

Nathan's face fell. His shoulders sagged. "We didn't want to take him, but he wouldn't let Gates go on his own."

"Tarrin was protecting Gates?" Selena shook her head. "You had no right to take either of the boys. Gates was innocent too."

"We had no choice." Nathan's voice was defiant. "It was the only way to retaliate."

Catal led Selena to a sofa. "If you were angry with me or the Walters, you didn't need to take the boys."

"Steve Walters deserves everything he gets." Mike spat the words out. "He broke Nathan's camera. He thought an apology would do, but that camera was irreplaceable."

"It was just an object." Selena's voice was low with confusion. "He gave your brother a new one, which was much more expensive than the one he broke."

"Our father gave that camera to Nathan." Mike's voice cracked. "He's dead now and that was the only thing we had to remember him by. So Steve can apologize all he wants, but now he's lost something that is irreplaceable too."

"There's no way you can compare a child with a camera." Her voice held a hint of hysteria.

Catal sat on the couch beside her and touched her arm. A sizzle of electricity went through him as he sent comfort and reassurance to Selena. He was a man used to killing, but he couldn't understand how anyone could harm a child or cause a woman pain. It was against everything he held sacred. These men needed to die, but not until they found out what they had done with the boys.

Selena looked up at him, begging him with her eyes to help. His stomach clenched at the anguish there. He brushed a strand of hair from her face just as her shoulders started to shake. Her tears came in a flood of grief and he pulled her close to his chest. He felt her devastation and he rocked her back and forth trying to ease the sorrow Mike's words had caused.

"Where are the boys?" Partlan's stern voice boomed through the room.

"I don't have to tell you anything," Nathan said with a sneer. "I don't even know who you are."

"You know me." Selena pulled away from Catal. "How could you hurt young boys?"

"We didn't injure anyone." Mike's voice was apologetic. "Honest. We don't have the stomach for it."

"What did you do then?" Catal's voice was a roar.

He jumped up from the couch. His patience was at an end. These men had taunted and pained Selena enough. They spoke in riddles, and he wanted answers, even if he had to kill one of them to get at the truth.

Mike shrugged. "I know my rights. We're not speaking to you without a lawyer present."

Catal picked Mike up from the chair. He grabbed his neck and pushed him against the wall. His fingers bit into the man's throat.

"We are not the police." Catal's voice was a low threat. "You have harmed a child and the code we live by says I have the right to shake you until you're dead. Maybe your brother will talk when I throw your limp body at his feet."

Mike's eyes bulged from his face. He struggled in Catal's grasp, but there was no release. His fingers pulled at Catal's hands, but it was futile. His feet were at least a foot from the floor, and he tried to kick out at Catal, but he evaded him. His face was blue before Nathan yelled.

"We sold them."

Partlan who had been watching with his arms crossed, frowned. "What does that mean? I did not think you had slavery in this country."

"Oh my god." Selena's body shook.

Catal glanced at her. Horror and disbelief were written over her face. He dropped Mike to the floor and went to her side.

He clasped her close. "It means they've sold them to people who will probably harm them."

"Explain." Partlan continued to look at Catal.

Catal cleared his throat. He glanced down at Selena and smoothed a hand across her back. She sighed and turned her face away from the brothers. He knew the others would find it impossible to believe. It was something that was foreign in Cygnus, yet all too common on Earth. He had never understood how a being could do that to another, especially a child.

"The boys will probably be traumatized for life."

There were several seconds of silence before Partlan spoke. "Is this true?"

Partlan leaned over Nathan. He was inches away from the photographer and his stance was threatening. Selena shivered beneath his hand. The brothers were monsters. Only the fact that they still needed information from them, kept Catal from ripping them apart with his bare hands.

Malac, who was rummaging through the brother's suitcases, pulled out a black backpack. "Here is the ransom money."

"So they are the kidnappers." Selena's voice was weak.

That settled it for Catal. There was no denying the guilt of these men. They had taken the boys, extorted money, and sold them. They were going to die.

Ranon shouted from the dining room. "I've found their computer. They've been receiving a number of suspicious emails in the past few days."

Partlan stood away from Nathan. "Move and I will kill you."

Nathan's eyes bulged. "You can't hurt me."

"I am not the police." Partlan spoke in a soft voice. "My job is to kill."

Nathan looked over at Selena. "You can't be serious?"

Selena nodded. "They are mercenaries that I hired. Now that I know what you've done with my son, I don't care what they do to you."

"And we will get the boys back." Catal's voice was a menace. "It was foolish to try and run. There is nowhere in the world that you can hide from us."

"The FBI wouldn't just let you come here and do this. I'll sue you." Mike rubbed his neck. "Good luck trying to get any information from us. The boys are lost to you forever."

"I might as well kill you now." Catal grabbed his gun from behind his back and pointed it at Mike. He cocked the hammer back and aimed.

"Stop." Nathan screamed at the top of his lungs. "The name of our contact is in one of our emails. He didn't give us his real name, though. That's all we know, honest."

Catal lowered the gun. "Where did you meet him?"

"Los Amigos Mall in South Central LA. It's on East Jefferson Boulevard. That's where we set up the exchange. We couldn't let the boys go home because they knew who we were, and we couldn't kill them." The words spilled from Nathan.

"So you thought you'd sell them?" Catal didn't hide his disgust.

"At least they'd be alive." Mike's voice was gruff.

Catal fought the urge to strangle the man. Instead he prodded Nathan in the back with his gun "When did you give him the boys?"

"Today. He met us at our storage unit. We don't know where the guy lives, honest."

"And you thought you'd got away with it?" Selena shook her head. "How did you expect to live with yourselves afterwards?"

Mike shrugged. "That's a lot of money. We could live like kings in another country. Then we would be the ones people would look up to and follow around."

"Not once they found out what you'd done to get that money." Catal rolled his eyes.

"That wouldn't have happened. Even the FBI were fooled by us." Nathan chuckled. "That tipoff to the other paparazzi was brilliant."

"Not brilliant enough." Catal shoved his pistol back into his waistband. "We found you."

"How long ago did you exchange the boys?" Partlan was gathering papers and computers from the dining room. He shoved them into a large suitcase that he emptied out on the floor.

"Right after the ransom drop." Nathan glanced over at his brother. "We couldn't keep the kids in the storage locker any longer. It was too hot."

"How did you find these guys?" Catal picked up a backpack and started stuffing photos in it.

"On the internet." Nathan shrugged. "We've got them some photos in the past, so it seemed like an easy exchange."

"What did you exchange?"

"New identities."

Partlan glanced at Catal. "*It would be best if Selena did not witness this.*"

Partlan went over to Nathan and started patting down his pockets. He pulled out a passport and threw it at Catal. Then, he went to Mike and did the same thing.

Catal put the passports into the inside pocket of his leather jacket. He zipped up the backpack and threw it on his back before walking over to Selena. He held out a hand.

"I'll take you to the van now."

"You're not going to kill them." Her fingers trembled in his. "I know I said I didn't care what happened, but I do. Let the law take care of them."

Catal kissed her hand before giving it a reassuring squeeze. "We have to gather more information. Time is important if we are to get the boys before any harm is done. We will leave the brothers for the police if that is your command."

Selena took a deep breath and stood up. "I trust you."

A surge of love went through Catal. Selena's words gave him strength. He felt the bond between them grow. He had denied the possibility of a pair bond because he'd doubted. Now he understood how powerful the connection between them could be. He already sensed her emotions. Soon they would know each other's thoughts. He led her out of the house and into the van.

Firbin was still at the wheel.

"Keep her here."

Catal closed the door and went back into the house. Partlan was zipping up the suitcase, and Ranon had two laptops under his arms. He walked over to Nathan and crossed his arms. "Selena wishes you to stand trial."

"We're going to tell the police everything you did to us." Mike's voice was a whine. "You'll be the ones behind bars."

"They have to find us first."

Partlan pulled plastic handcuffs from his jacket and pulled Mike's arms behind the chair back. "You are lucky. If a woman had not stood up for you, I would have killed you with my bare hands."

Mike's eyes widened. "You wouldn't get away with it."

"A Hunter does what he wants, especially when the Sacred Code is broken." Partlan put duct tape over Mike's mouth.

Catal secured Nathan's arms behind his chair. "Where is your storage unit?"

Nathan shrugged. "I've told you everything I'm going to. If you guys are so good, you can find it yourself. You already have our computers."

Catal's jaw tightened. "We'll find it."

"It won't do you any good." Nathan's voice was sulky. "We don't know the name of the man we sold the boys to. It's a big organization and no one knows who the others are. It's safer that way. That's all I'm going to say."

Partlan taped Nathan's mouth. There was no point in wasting any more time with these men. They had their computers and the storage unit information would be on it. They should be able to find the man who took the boys from there.

Partlan lifted Mike from his chair and moved him into the dining room. He put another plastic handcuff around the radiator and then attached it to one of Mike's wrists. Malac dragged Nathan in and attached him in the same way to the opposite side of the heating unit. There would be no chance of them breaking the cuffs away from the strong metal.

They would be uncomfortable, but they would be alive. When it was safe, they would contact the FBI and let them know what they'd found. Who knew, maybe the FBI's surveillance would lead them to the brothers before they notified them.

Ranon left with the computers. Catal made certain the doors were locked and then waited outside for Partlan.

"It's not wise to keep them alive." Catal kept his voice low.

"It is what she wishes." Partlan shut the door. "There is no real harm in leaving them here. They have no money and even if they get free, they will not go far without identification."

Catal clenched his hands into fists. He knew what Selena wanted, but he was still a Hunter. "If the boys aren't alive, I will come back and kill them."

"I will join you, but now we need to concentrate on finding the boys." Partlan's voice was unemotional. "Once we have the storage unit, we should be able to follow the trail."

They walked to the van. The cool air of the night surrounded them and Catal inhaled deeply. He needed to clear his head and focus on finding the boys. Their kidnappers were secure. There was no way that the brothers would escape justice. Partlan was right. They had to follow Selena's wishes.

Breanon joined them once they reached the van. The unit was complete. Now the work of tracking began again. They drove for several miles until they reached a small motel off of Hollywood Boulevard. The motel had seen better days, but it would satisfy their needs. They took two adjoining rooms and started setting up the computers. Catal threw the backpack on one of the beds and pulled the passports out of his jacket.

"These might give us a lead as to who they were in contact with." Catal opened the papers. "They are good fakes. There are only a few people in the country that can do this kind of work."

"That's a start." Partlan turned to Firbin. "I need the location of the storage unit. Once I have that, then we are going to take a trip there. Surveillance cameras might have picked up the exchange."

Selena inhaled a sharp breath. Catal turned to see her face go pale. He cursed himself for a fool. They had been talking so matter of fact about something that was painful. He touched her arm.

"You need to rest."

"Catal, take her into the other room. You need to care for your mate. We can handle this." Partlan's instructions were a soft murmur in his mind.

Catal took Selena's arm and steered her into the other room. He closed the adjoining door and led her to the bed. The room was clean and with the door shut, the outside world seemed to fade away. It was perfect.

Selena cleared her throat. "I need to tell you something."

Chapter 13

"It's about Tarrin."

Selena sat on the bed and looked up at Catal who stood a few feet away. A frisson of heat sparked between them. She inhaled a sharp breath and clasped her hands together. She needed to tell him the truth. It had to be done before she could consider a future with Catal, and that was what she wanted more than anything. Once Tarrin was found, she wanted all of them to become a family.

"Tell me." Catal crouched down in front of her.

Selena choked back a sob. This was more difficult than she'd anticipated. The words were stuck in her throat. All these years she had held her secret tight to her heart, never daring to remember the love that had created her son. All she could do was start at the beginning, as painful as the memories were.

"I came to the United States as a refugee. It was very hard to find employment until I met Nikki. She gave me a home and security."

"She protected you and was your friend." Catal's voice was solemn. "I will always be grateful to her for that."

"I didn't find out I was pregnant until I was living here."

"You took another mate." Catal nodded. "I can understand that. Where is this man? Why is he not by your side now?"

"There is no other man." Selena looked into Catal's eyes and saw the confusion there. "There has never been anyone but you."

Catal's eyes widened. "You mean you didn't mate with another? You waited for me?"

"You are the only man I have ever loved." Selena exhaled a shaky breath. "You are also the only one I have ever hated. Do you forgive me?"

"Always."

"I was spoiled, confused, and selfish. I acted like an inconsiderate child instead of an adult."

Selena cringed inwardly at what a fool she'd been to run. She should have waited and talked to Catal, but at the time she didn't think he was ever coming back for her. That didn't excuse her from not telling him about Tarrin. The very least she could have done was try and find him after she'd learned that she was pregnant.

"There's no defence for what I did."

"You're perfect." Catal's voice was sincere. "You have always been."

"No." Selena shook her head. "When I found out I was pregnant, I chose not to contact you. My decision caused you to lose seven years of Tarrin's life. You have every right to hate me."

Catal brought her hands to his mouth. A shiver of awareness and desire sparked through her. The wonder of it stopped her breath. She had never thought she'd feel this way again.

"We are joined." Catal's voice was a husky vow. "There is nothing you could ever do that would destroy the pair bond."

"Do you understand what I am saying?" Selena's fingers tensed in his hand.

Catal frowned. "You regret running from me. What more do I need to understand?"

"I said that you were the only man I had ever been with."

Selena paused for several seconds. Catal looked at her with a blank stare.

"I'm trying to tell you that I have never made love with another man." Selena cleared her throat. "Tarrin is your son."

Selena held her breath and waited for Catal's anger.

Instead, he frowned. "How is that possible?"

"It happens when a man and a woman are intimate. And we were frequently intimate."

"But Hunters cannot have children."

"Who told you that?" Selena reached up and touched Catal on the shoulder. A shiver of awareness raced up her arm. "You are the only man I have ever made love with. There is no other possible father."

Catal sat on the bed beside her. He ran his hands through his hair and shook his head. "How can this be? It's contrary to what we've been told."

"Nevertheless, it's the truth." Selena squeezed his hand. "I know it's a shock to find out this way, but you are Tarrin's father."

"It means Tarrin is a Hunter." He turned to her and smiled. "We may have a chance to track him."

"Now I'm the one who's confused." Selena frowned. "We still don't know who the men are that bought the boys."

"We may be able to mind connect." Catal's voice was serious. "There's a chance that Tarrin will be able to hear other Hunters."

Selena searched Catal's face for some indication of what he meant. All she saw there was hope. She didn't have a clue what he was talking about, but the confidence she saw in his eyes gave her courage. Catal had already admitted that he wasn't from Earth. Perhaps there were more secrets.

Secrets that could save their son's life.

"What is mind connect?"

"You are my pair bond." Catal's voice was a low whisper. "Before you closed your mind to me, we were linked. Do you remember?"

Selena searched her memories for that wonderful three months she had spent with Catal. She was confined to the compound for most of the time. The guerrilla activity had increased and many neighbors in the area had tightened their security. Every day she woke up knowing that she'd see Catal, though. Her world had revolved around him. That's why her brother's insistence that he had betrayed her, had cut so deep.

They would steal away for hours and make love. Life had been dangerous, but in the midst of the fears, was the bond that she had with Catal. It was as if he could read her mind. His thoughts and feelings were hers. They shared everything.

"We were in love." Her words were hesitant. "We were always together. You protected me and saved my life more than once."

"I sensed when you were in danger." Catal picked up her hand and kissed it. "I was a fool not to believe in the bonding, but I didn't understand."

"So there is more to our connection than what you told me?"

Catal gaze became intense. "A Hunter is bred to be the best warrior possible. He is bred to obey and protect."

"You are fierce fighters. Even Juan was surprised at how good your unit was."

"Remember, I told you that we were genetically modified and had implants to strengthen us?" When Selena nodded, Catal continued. "Those same implants prevented us from pair bonding. It was forbidden for a Hunter to have a mate."

"You weren't allowed to mate ever?" Selena tilted her head. "You certainly seemed quite capable when we were together."

"You had never been with another man. If you had, you might have known how inexperienced I was." Catal's tone was wry. "You were the only woman I had ever been drawn to. From the moment I saw you standing beside your brother, I knew you were different."

"How so?"

"I wanted to be with you." Catal's eyes softened. "It was more than an attraction. It was a soul searing need. It was as important to me as breathing. Every second of the day, I craved and yearned to be with you. I had lived on your planet for over twenty years and never once had that happened to me. As far as I knew, it hadn't occurred to any of my fellow brothers either."

"Never?" Selena's voice was uncertain.

Catal shook his head. "I thought being surrounded by humans made us immune to you. We are not from this planet, and even though we look similar, we are different. Lorcan was our leader, and he held all humans in contempt. We did what we had to survive, but there were no thoughts of interaction with you."

"So there was no attraction for you to women."

"None. It was thought impossible and beneath a Hunter to even look at a woman." Catal looked down at their joined hands. "All that changed the moment I met you. I risked everything I held sacred being with you. If my fellow Hunters had found out, I thought I would have been cut off from them."

Selena swallowed. She hadn't realized that Catal had jeopardized so much by being with her. When her brother had told her that Catal was responsible for the massacre of their men, she had felt humiliated and a fool. She'd believed everything they'd shared had been a lie. She thought he had used her. Running away had been a childish reaction, but it had kept her sane. She couldn't bear to dwell on what had happened. Later, when Tarrin had been born, she'd been forced to fend for both of them. It had forced her to mature.

"You broke the rules by being with me."

"I threw away the rules. I disobeyed orders to be with you. There was nothing that could stop me. You are my pair bond. I didn't understand then, but I do now. That is why it is forbidden for us to mate."

"Men can have wives and still do their jobs." Selena's chest tightened with sympathy. "They don't have to choose one over the other."

"A Hunter does." Catal closed his eyes briefly. "Our genetic modifications mean that our loyalty and allegiance is narrow. Once bonded, we put our mate above all else, even our orders. When you ran away, I stayed in Colombia searching for you for months after the rest of the unit left. I blocked all communication with my fellow brothers and ignored my leader's directives."

Selena's breath caught in her throat. She hadn't realized to what lengths Catal had gone to find her. "Your family should come first. They must have understood that."

"Not for a warrior. We are bred to fight and die, nothing more. I never told my fellow Hunters why I had left. When I returned, they assumed I'd been injured. There is no other acceptable justification for my disobedience."

"That's horrible. There is more to life than war and death."

"Perhaps, but that is a Hunter's purpose." Catal's voice was harsh. "We do the work that others don't have the stomach for. It's a brutal world, and even though I've lived most of my life on Earth, nothing has changed that fact."

"So there is no room for love."

Catal shook his head. "No."

"Then what happened between us?"

"My implants probably malfunctioned, or were turned off when I was captured by the military. Other Hunters who have crashed here recently, have found mates. Their implants were disconnected months before they came to Earth." Catal shrugged. "That is the only reason I have, because none of the other warriors that were stranded on Earth at the same time as me, have ever found a mate.

"Perhaps they did, but refused to talk about it."

"I would know." Catal squeezed her hand. "We communicate in ways that humans do not. That is what I've been trying to explain."

"Mind connect?" Selena raised an eyebrow. "Are you saying that you know what each other is thinking all the time?"

"Not all the time, but we can connect telepathically. This is something we never told our handlers or teachers. It is only known among Hunters."

"It's a secret."

"Yes." Catal's voice was firm. "Well guarded. It gives us an advantage in battle. We can converse at great distances with each other."

"Why are you telling me then?"

"That same communication is possible between mates."

Shock ripped through Selena. "We never had that."

"I never trusted fully." Catal's voice was apologetic. "If I had understood the bonding it would have been different. Perhaps then you might have known that I would never have betrayed you. To deceive you would have been like killing myself."

"I know we were close, but I never heard your voice in my head."

"No, but often I could make you happy when you were sad." Catal gave her a crooked smile. "It is something I have tried to do throughout this kidnapping ordeal. I've sent you my love and strength."

Selena bit her lip. His efforts hadn't been in vain. She had sensed his support frequently. Sometimes it had been so strong that she had thought he was actually holding her in his arms. That part of the bonding had been real.

"Will we be able to speak to each other telepathically one day?"

"If we trust, yes." Catal pulled her close. "For eight years, I've been nothing but a shell of a man. Having known one's mate and then to lose her, is worse than anything else. It is hell. Death would be preferable. The only reason I continued is that I hoped one day I would find you. That you would lower your defenses and let me in again."

"Is that all it takes?" Selena's voice was doubtful. "After so many years, all I have to do is open myself up to you?"

"Yes." Catal looked down at her. "You have the power, not me. If you want to strengthen the bond, then it will be so."

Selena reached up and brushed her hand over his forehead. He shivered at her touch, a soft moan escaped his lips. She tilted her head and let her fingers drift down the side of his face. His skin was rough from a couple of days of stubble, sending tingles of sensation throughout her body.

This was the man she had always loved.

The only man for her.

She leaned up and touched his lips with hers. Instant fire exploded. Catal clung for a second and then his mouth moved over hers. Sensations and desires that she had long thought dead came to life. She leaned into him and let her body lead the way.

His tongue glided over hers, sending flutters of heat throughout her. She twisted in his arms until she found the position where she fit perfectly. Her body remembered. This was heaven, and for several seconds, she let the world fade away while she luxuriated in the protection of Catal.

All too soon the kiss ended. She stared up into his eyes and almost cried at the love she saw there. He was her other half. He completed her. He had always been her mate, and she'd been a fool to deny it.

"We can't change that." His voice was a husky whisper. "We have today and the rest of our lives."

"How did you know what I was thinking?"

"Our bond is growing strong." Catal gave her a light kiss. "You have lowered your guard and let me in again."

"Is this how it was before?" Selena's lips clung to his. "Did you always know what I was thinking?"

"No." Catal sighed. "I didn't trust. I thought that pair bonding was only a legend. Can you forgive me for doubting and not being totally honest with you?"

Selena nodded and moved away. "Yes. My sin is greater than yours. I denied you Tarrin."

"You were protecting him." Catal grimaced. "I failed you. It was my duty to keep you safe and I didn't. It was my fault."

"That's because I shut you out of our lives." Selena fought back her tears. "You didn't know where to find me."

"That was your right to deny me." Catal's voice was gentle. "I accepted your decision. I wanted to find you so that I could tell you the truth about myself. You deserved to know that I would always be there for you, no matter what."

"Not telling you about Tarrin was inexcusable." Selena's tears started to fall. "It was the cruelest thing I could have done."

Catal shook his head. "You are not to blame. On my planet, women make all of the decisions. Men do not expect to be considered. Our children are not raised the same on Cygnus. Remember, I told you that Hunters are created in birthing chambers?

Selena nodded. "It sounds barbaric."

"This is the same for all children on Cygnus. Women do not give birth to children."

"Do mothers take care of their babies?"

"Children do not have parents. They grow up in learning institutions until they are deemed ready." Catal's voice held regret. "That is one of the things I most admire about humans. They create family units and nurture their offspring. On Cygnus, you become what your genes have been programed for."

Selena shivered at how cold and sterile the surroundings must be. Laughter and play would be impossible in an environment where the goal was teaching and preparing children for their responsibilities as adults. They'd be expected to learn quickly and then leave to fulfill their duties.

It was hard enough to image Catal's childhood. He'd been raised to fight and die. At least he had his brother Hunters to bond with. A whole society where people were genetically created for one purpose, was calculating and unemotional. She was thankful Catal had escaped. Together, they would give Tarrin choices in his life.

"You have a family now." Selena reached up and kissed him. "You have me, and Tarrin, your son."

"Is he truly mine?" Catal's voice held awe. "He is a Hunter?"

"Yes." Selena smiled. "Every day he grows more and more like you. The things he says, and his actions, remind me of you. He's the younger one, but he protects Gates. You heard the Gordon brothers. Tarrin was only kidnapped because he refused to let Gates be taken alone."

"That may be the way we can save the boys."

"I don't understand."

Catal stood and straightened his shoulders. "Tarrin is a Hunter. That means we may be able to reach him through mind connection. If he has been keeping track of his location, then we should find the boys."

Selena's heart fluttered. Was it possible? Could Catal connect with Tarrin?

"It is possible." Catal stood and pulled the bedcovers back. "You need to sleep. You are exhausted."

"Are you reading my mind again?" Selena wiped the tears off her cheek with her finger and crawled under the sheets. "When will I be able to read yours?"

"*You can do it now. I will always let you hear my thoughts.*" Catal went to the door.

Selena's body jerked. Catal's words were in her head. He hadn't spoken aloud. He was right. They were connected in a way that only the two of them would ever know. A warm glow of happiness infused her. Did he know how much she loved him?

"Yes." Catal smiled and then opened the door. "Partlan, I have information that might help the search."

Chapter14

He was a father.

His heart was pounding in his chest and a warm heat radiated through his body. The world shone brighter. He had the answer to saving the boys. He didn't know how Partlan and the others would handle the news he had to give them, but it could only be positive. Never in his wildest dreams had he ever thought he would father a child. With the genetic modifications and the implants he'd been given, it should have been impossible. Hunters only had one purpose and that was fighting.

No one on Cygnus had children.

It wasn't biologically needed any longer.

He had often watched human families and marveled at their resilience. Adults and children communicating together was foreign to most warriors. Because he had grown up on Earth, he'd had ample opportunity to observe the interaction of parents and youngsters. He'd wondered how it would feel to have a parent protect and watch over you. When they had crashed on Earth, they'd been deserted by their teachers and then set upon by government agencies that hunted them. They were children set adrift in a strange land. It would have been comforting to have a family.

Now he had one.

Selena and Tarrin were his family.

"What have you discovered?" Partlan looked up as Catal entered the room.

Catal shut the door with a quiet click. He walked into the room. Malac and Firbin were busy at computers, while Breanon had spread a map over one of the beds. Ranon was sorting through papers and photos on the other bed with Partlan.

He cleared his throat. "Selena has finally opened up to me. She has given me information that I find unbelievable, but it's true."

"What is that?" Firbin looked up from his computer. "Will it help with finding the boys?"

Catal nodded. "I believe so. Tarrin is my son. He is a Hunter."

Silence followed his announcement.

Firbin was the first to speak. His eyes were wide and his voice low. "How is this possible? Hunters do not have children."

"We weren't supposed to have mates either." Catal smiled. "Despite the odds against it happening, it is the truth."

"It seems we are more compatible with humans than we thought." Partlan's voice was dry. "I think both Ardal and Niail need to know this."

Ardal, their leader, needed to be made aware of the situation. His mate Fiona, was a doctor. If anyone could explain how this happened, she would. It might be an aberration restricted to him. Niail, a member of Ardal's unit that had crashed on Earth recently, had just found his mate Kimi. She already had two children, so it was essential that they know whether Niail was capable of being a father too.

"We may be able to connect with Tarrin." Catal's voice was positive.

"And let him tell us where they are being kept? It is a good idea, but the boy might be unable to communicate with us. He is also part human." Partlan went to the computer that Firbin was working on. "We have found some information."

Firbin moved his fingers over the keys. "We know where the Gordon brother's storage unit is located. They said that they had hid the boys there and it is where the exchange happened."

Catal leaned over Firbin's shoulder. "The unit is not far from here."

"Do they have security cameras?"

"Yes." Firbin pointed to a picture of the gated front of the storage units. "It is an outdated system so it is not online. We will have to go and get the footage. That is the only way for us to view what is on it."

"We should leave now." Catal straightened up. "Selena has just gone to sleep. She won't know we've gone. If we're quick, then we will have the information we need and be back before she awakens."

"Malac and Ranon can stay behind." Partlan picked up his jacket. "They will continue searching for any mention of these groups that abduct children."

Catal's stomach tightened. Bile rose in his throat at the thought of what might be happening to the boys. With a shock, he realized he was afraid. The emotion was new to him. A Hunter never considered what might happen to him during battle. He was prepared and trained to die. The thought of something happening to Tarrin or Selena, terrified him. It was paralyzing in its grip. He inhaled a sharp breath and forced his mind to concentrate on the rescue.

"These people are adept at hiding their activities from the law."

"We cannot waste any time." Partlan went to the door. "On the way to the unit, you can try and connect with Tarrin. He might not understand what is happening at first. You may have to make several attempts before you connect."

Catal nodded and they left the hotel. Once they were in the van he focused his thoughts on Tarrin. He pulled out the picture Selena had given him and reached out with his mind.

Nothing.

It was as if he were trying to penetrate a brick wall.

He glanced up at Partlan who was sitting beside him and shook his head. "He is either incapable of hearing us, or is blocking the connection."

"It might not be that." Partlan lowered his voice. "This is a boy who never knew about you. He does not have a clue that this type of communication is possible. It may take a while before you can connect, but you have to keep trying."

Catal nodded. "Does Ardal know?"

"I've told him. He was surprised, like you, but he said it explains some things. Fiona is going to investigate it. After we rescue the boys, you will meet up with him and Niail." Partlan leaned close. "You three are the only Hunters with human mates, so you all need to understand why you have been able to father a child. Ardal should have answers by then."

Catal exhaled. Everything was different for them on Earth. He had refused to accept that pair bonds was real. Even after mating with Selena, he had still doubted. It wasn't until Ardal had found his own mate that he'd learned to believe. He didn't need to know the reason behind his ability to father a child, to accept the truth. He was a father, and soon he would find his son.

Firbin eased the van to a stop.

He parked across the road from the storage units. It was a dimly lit area, with several of the street lights flickering on and off. It added a surreal element to the street. A ten foot rod-iron gate blocked the building's entrance. There was a chain and lock around the gate, and two cameras mounted on the side of the building beyond the gates.

No other security was in sight. Any surveillance equipment would be in the main office. They would have to scale the fence and break into the office to get the tapes.

Partlan nodded to Breanon. Breanon grabbed his assault rifle and left the van. He would take up a position that would give him full view of the storage area and main office. No one should be able to get inside without him knowing. He was their lookout.

Catal picked up a pistol and pushed it into the inside pocket of his jacket. He took a second gun and put it in the waistband at the back of his jeans. When he was ready, he heaved a deep breath and then followed Partlan out of the van. Firbin would stay and have the vehicle ready for their escape.

The fence looked to be wired.

Catal threw a stone at it and nothing happened.

No electricity flowed through it. They just had to climb it. Partlan went first. Catal jumped over the top and landed on the pavement beside him. The low thud of his boots hitting the ground reverberated through the air. They waited a few seconds.

Silence.

No one responded to their intrusion.

They ran in a crouching position to the rear of the facility. There were long rows of buildings with garage doors on either side. Chains and locks secured the doors. The dull glare of the spotlights added a grey tinge to the units. They went past three rows of buildings before they came to a stop. It was a long corridor that held units in both directions. Partlan turned right, Catal went left.

The office was at the end of Catal's side.

He looked through a window.

It was dark inside.

"*I'm here*," he advised Partlan.

He tried the handle, but it was locked. By the time he had pulled out his lock pick set, Partlan had joined him. A couple of twists and turns and the door opened. Partlan went in first, gun in hand as he checked the two roomed office. It was empty.

Catal rummaged the desk and shelf area in the first room, but there was no taping or surveillance equipment. He turned the computer on and started to search through their files while Partlan explored the back room. Catal found the list of tenants and sent a copy to Malac at the hotel. The rest of the files were correspondence and financials. Nothing significant stood out.

"The security equipment is back here."

Catal shut down the computer and went into the rear office. There was an antiquated camera system with video tape recorders and several monitors. Rows of tapes were stored in a bookshelf. Catal picked one of them up. It was a specialized tape that recorded for at least twelve hours. The quality wouldn't be good, but that could be enhanced.

"The Gordon's rented Unit 167. It's in the third row on the left." Catal pointed to the monitor that was fixed along that side. "The exchange took place today so it should have been recorded on the tape in the machine."

Partlan rewound the tape machine and started to play back the recording for that monitor. They sped through the images until they noticed Nathan Gordon enter the facility. They followed him to his unit. He was met there by a tall, dark-haired man driving a black sedan. The vehicle pulled up in front of the storage unit. The man got out of the car and popped the trunk open. Then he went into the unit with Nathan.

Several minutes later, he was carrying a bundle of material. He threw it into the trunk. Nathan followed him with what looked like a rolled up area rug that also went into the trunk. The men shook hands and then the dark haired one drove off. Nathan locked the unit and left.

Partlan rewound the tape.

He paused it when the vehicle came in sight.

"Is there any way to magnify the image?" Partlan's eyes didn't leave the screen.

"I'll send a copy to Malac. He should be able to clean it up."

Catal looked around the office for connection cords and then hooked up the computer sitting on the desk. His fingers flew across the keyboard as he set up a program to record the image from the monitor. He saved it and then emailed that to Malac. He then erased all he had done and put the computer back in place.

"The police are going to need the evidence here to prosecute the Gordon brothers so we'll leave it in place." Catal pulled the cords from the rear of the tape machine. "Malac can examine the vehicle. A license plate will give us a location."

"Good." Partlan pointed at the monitor. "Erase the footage of us entering the warehouses."

Catal nodded. "I'll erase that portion of the tape and leave the recorders off. The FBI won't have any evidence of us entering or leaving."

When he was done, they left the office as silently as they had entered. Firbin had the van running when they returned. Breanon took his seat in the front. There was very little conversation as they drove back to the motel. The next step would depend on whether Malac was able to get any information from the video Catal had sent him.

Ranon and Malac were both leaning over a computer when they came in.

"Any luck?" Catal couldn't keep the tension from his voice.

"We are piecing together the license number." Malac didn't bother to look up. "Ranon has hacked into the vehicle registry website. Once I have enough numbers, we will run them."

Partlan went to the second computer and pulled up the video of the man that the brothers were talking to. It was difficult to see his face because he never looked directly into the camera. His height and body shape would be useful to compare to the registry lists.

"Is Selena still asleep?" Catal glanced toward the closed connecting door.

"She has been there the whole time you were away." Ranon's voice was low. "We did not think it was right to go into the room."

"It's probably best."

Catal straightened up and went to the door. He cracked it open a few inches and looked inside. His stomach clenched when he saw Selena curled up on the bed. She had thrown the blankets off and her knees were tight against her chest. He went in and covered her up, brushing a finger down her cheek before he left.

He still had a hard time believing that she was here with him. The years of silence had convinced him that he would remain alone for the rest of his life. To be given a second chance with Selena was more than he had hoped for. It was enough to know that she was alive. It was better than the agony of believing her dead. He would have died himself if that had been the case.

He gave her one last look and then moved away with a sigh. There was work to do. Finding Tarrin before something horrible happened was all that mattered now. Time was not a luxury they had.

He closed the door with a soft click and then returned to the computer Malac was working on.

"I have five of the numbers and letters." Malac's voice was excited. "That is enough to take a run through the vehicle registration."

"Give them to me." Partlan was ready to input the data.

"K23 blank 27."

"We have three possible vehicles." Partlan's voice hesitated at he scanned the computer screen. "Only one fits the car. It's for a David Hendry. He lives on Pauma Valley Drive in Porter Ranch."

"How far is that?"

"It is about forty minutes away, but at this time of night it should be quicker."

"We had best head out."

"Where are you going?" Selena's voice interrupted their packing up.

Catal turned around to look at her. The sight of her caused his heart to beat faster. She was beautiful, even with the grogginess of sleep. He still couldn't believe that he had lived for years without her. It hurt too much to think what might happen if he didn't find Tarrin. He doubted either of them would be able to continue on.

"We've a lead on who might have taken the boys."

"Then I want to come."

"It could be dangerous." Partlan picked up a pistol. "Ranon can stay here with you while we are gone."

"I need to be there." Selena walked into the room. "What if you find the boys? They'll want to see a familiar face. I don't want to complain, but you guys would scare them to death."

Catal gave her a crooked smile. "Good. We want to be certain we scare the men holding them too."

"No problem there." Selena moved back into the bedroom. "I'm getting my stuff and coming with you."

"As you wish." Partlan shrugged. "We will all go. Pack up everything. If we have to follow the boys out of the city, then I do not want to waste time coming back here."

The work was finished in a few minutes. Ranon went down and paid the bill, and then they left. They took the freeway and were outside of David Hendry's residence within thirty minutes. It was a large house on a double lot. There was a red brick wall that blocked the driveway from the neighbors. Trees and hedges along the front street gave the house complete privacy.

Firbin drove into the driveway, past the brick wall, and parked. The dark vehicle from the storage unit's video tape was pulled up to the front door of the house. Catal forced his anger down. He needed a clear head to deal with this man. Anger would only interfere. They all drew their guns, put silencers on them, and waited for Partlan's command.

"Firbin stay in the vehicle with Selena. If anyone comes out, stop them." Partlan nodded to the rest of them. "You know the operation. Surround the house and wait for my orders."

Catal reached over and squeezed Selena's hands. "If the boys are here, we'll find them."

He jumped out of the van and followed the others. He skirted around the side of the house. A golf course ran behind the dwelling. The yard had a swimming pool and again a heavily hedged and treed lot that blocked others from looking in. The windows of the house had dark curtains drawn across them. Not even shadows could be seen on the outside. No one would ever know if there were illegal activities going on in this house.

Partlan motioned for him to move.

Catal eased the screen door open.

There was no sound from inside. He tried the handle on the wooden door. It turned. With a flick of his wrist he opened it and entered the house. Everywhere there was darkness. He inhaled and eased his breathing before walking down the hall.

It was too convenient.

There was no way to miss the sound of a car coming up the drive. He was expecting them. Catal waited at the first door opening. Partlan entered the house behind him. When they were together Catal jumped around the opening into the room. It was the kitchen.

It was empty.

Partlan took the lead at the next opening. He entered and came back out shaking his head. That left the main living area of the house and a hallway that probably led to the bedrooms. There was one closed door that was either a closet or the basement. There was a lock on the door. They would leave that until the last.

They waited.

Breanon had set up outside the house from a location that let him see anyone coming and going. So their man couldn't escape without them knowing. Malac and Ranon were at the front entrance.

"*Try the door.*" Partlan sent his command to the men through mind connection.

"*It is locked.*"

Partlan glanced over at Catal. This was it. They had to take a chance. Their quarry was probably waiting for them, but it couldn't be helped. Catal took a deep breath and lowered his body into a crouch position. That should give him an element of surprise. The guy was probably expecting them to be standing.

He eased around the doorway.

A dull ping rang out, followed by a swooshing above his head.

Partlan returned fire.

A scream pierced the air. Their quarry was standing in the center of the room holding his hand. Blood was dripping onto the plush beige rug beneath his feet. Partlan had shot the gun out of the man's hand.

Catal jumped onto him and tackled him to the ground. Partlan stepped around them and opened the front door so that Malac and Ranon could enter. They closed the door behind them and pointed the gun at the man who was struggling with Catal on the ground.

"It is no use." Partlan's voice was severe. "Your house is surrounded. If you continue to struggle it will be easier for us to just kill you."

The man laughed. "You guys must be nuts. Do you know who you're dealing with?"

Catal hauled his prisoner up and then threw him into a chair. "Your connections can't help you now. They never could."

"Get me a bandage." The man squeezed his wounded hand. "I don't care what you do, I won't talk to you. I want my lawyer."

"You will talk." Partlan switched on a light. "They always do."

"You're nuts."

"We've come for the boys." Catal grabbed the man's shirt and shook him. "You're David Hendry and we know you bought them from the Gordon brothers."

"My operation depends on secrecy. You have nothing on me but allegations." The man pushed away from Catal. "I won't tell you a thing."

"Are the boys here?"

Just then the door opened and Selena walked into the room. The prisoner's eyes widened when he saw her. For a second he just stared and then he looked away. "Bringing her here won't change anything. I won't talk."

Partlan looked at Selena. "It would be best if you waited outside. We are going to have to use force. No woman should see that."

"I grew up in a military compound." Selena walked to the prisoner. "I'm aware of the methods used to get information from people. I prefer to use gentler means. I think they're just as effective."

"You think I'll talk?" David Hendry looked at Selena and laughed. "You're pretty sweetheart, but much too old for me."

She slapped him across the face. "Where is my son?"

The man shook his head. "You can search all you want, but you won't find him here. They're lost forever."

Chapter 15

Selena choked back her horror.

There was no way she was going to let this monster see how his words affected her. She had to be stronger than him. That was the only way to get information out of him. No personal feelings, no emotion. You had to keep the upper hand in an interrogation. If he saw your weakness, it would motivate him to resist questioning.

She narrowed her eyes. "What do you mean?"

"I'm not speaking anymore."

Catal punched him in the face. A trickle of blood slipped from between his lips. "Answer her."

"What are you, her underling?" The man snorted. "Who's in control here?"

Catal's leaned close to the man. "She is my mate and one of the boys you took is my son."

A shiver went through David Hendry.

"We protect our own." Catal raised an eyebrow. "We are warriors who seek justice. We are not law enforcement, so we have no rules to follow except our code of honor. We'll have the information from you that we need. The question is how long you will withstand the interrogation before you break."

"And you will break." Partlan went to Catal's side. "A Hunter is sworn to protect women and children, but also his fellow brothers. You have taken a child who is one of us. Death is the only thing you can hope for."

"You guys can't be for real." David gave a half choked laugh. "There are laws against what you're suggesting. Besides, I have friends who will hunt you down."

"We'll kill them first." Catal straightened away from David.

Selena shivered at the look of determination in Catal's eyes. She had witnessed him and his unit in battle many times. She knew there was no one equal to their skill or fierceness. She had never seen him in an interrogation, though. That was something her brother Juan handled. She didn't know if she would be able to stomach what had to be done to find Tarrin.

She straightened her shoulders.

Questioning David Hendry was necessary if she wanted her son back alive.

Catal touched her arm. "You should leave this to us. This man is weak and will break soon, but I don't want you witnessing it."

Selena looked at David and saw the wariness in his blue eyes. He was meticulously groomed and wearing a designer golf shirt and pants that had to cost a fortune. A hint of grey showed at his temples. His dark hair was cut short and he had a perfect two day's growth of beard shadowing his face. He could have walked off the pages of any men's magazine.

Catal had assessed the man's character correctly. He would tell them anything rather than endure pain. She didn't want to know what they had to do in order to get the information. All she wanted was her son. She'd asked the Hunters to help and she needed to let them do their job.

She turned to leave when David's voice stopped her. "Alright, I'll tell you where I took them, but it's not going to help you. The boys are gone."

Partlan kicked the man's foot. "Speak."

"They were too hot to keep in California." The man shrugged. "I mean their pictures are plastered everywhere, so I set them up for transportation out of state. I left them with a trucker we use in Castaic. He's already on the road by now."

"Where is he going?" Partlan took a step toward David.

"I don't know."

Partlan leaned close to David.

"Honest." David raised his voice. "That's part of the security of the network. No one knows what the next person does or where they go."

"What's the trucker's name?"

"I haven't a clue."

"So you expect us to believe you just handed the boys over to someone you didn't see, or speak to?" Partlan raised an eyebrow.

"I didn't say that." David's tone was sarcastic. "The man had a beard and was in his forties. He had a large belly and gray hair."

"What kind of truck did he drive?"

David shrugged. "How the hell would I know that? They all look the same to me. It was big. One of those semi-tractor trailers."

"Did it have a name on the side?"

David pursed his lips. "Diamond Frozen Foods or something like that."

"You put them in a freezer unit?" Partlan's voice was a low menace. "How did you expect them to survive?

Selena's breath caught in her throat. How could they throw two young children into a freezer and not even care what happened? They treated them as if they were inanimate objects and not living boys with feelings. Her stomach heaved at the evil of these people.

"How can you live with yourself?" Selena's voice caught in her throat. "You're a monster."

"I'm the middleman. I broker the deals, that's all. It's strictly business. What happens after I exchange them isn't my concern." David rolled his eyes at her and turned back to Partlan. He crossed his arms over his chest. "I've told you what I know, so you can leave now."

"That's not possible."

Partlan glanced at Catal and he in turn looked at her. Catal took her arm and pulled her close. "It's best we leave."

Selena looked at David and saw confusion in his eyes. "You could leave him for the police."

"We already did that with the Gordon brothers. This man has done damage to many children. He has no honor."

Selena bit her lip. "You can't just kill him."

"Yes. We can." Catal's voice was firm.

Selena let him lead her to the door. She knew that Catal was right. The man was a monster and his connections would probably ensure that he never saw jail time. In a few weeks, he'd be back in business and more children would be kidnapped. She couldn't live with herself if another child was harmed.

She turned back to look at David Hendry. The man's eyes narrowed at her glance and then he reached toward Partlan's gun. Partlan stopped his hand with his own. Both of them had hold of the pistol, pulling back and forth then. Partlan's face was impassive.

Partlan was bigger and stronger.

Hendry's hand was bent back and the pistol was aimed at his chest. Hendry grimaced as he struggled to deflect the weapon away from him. The gun jerked. The silent shot seemed more deafening than a normal blast. Hendry's eyes widened and he looked down. He'd been shot in the heart. A stain of bright red blood was seeping through the pink cotton of his shirt. The acrid smell of spent gunpowder filled the air.

Partlan was unhurt.

He pulled the pistol out of Hendry's hand and let him slump to the floor.

"It would have been better to have the names of the people he gave the boys to." Partlan shook his head.

"His computers and papers may lead us to them." Malac's voice was hopeful. "Should we search for the whereabouts of other missing children?"

"The police will take care of it. They have the resources to track down his network and arrest them." Partlan stepped away from the body. "Search the house. The boys may still be here."

Malac and Ranon left the room.

"Why haven't the neighbors ever called the police?" Selena went to the front door and looked out the decorative circular window at eye height. "Surely they've heard and seen things coming from this house?"

"My guess is the place has been soundproofed."

Catal went to the wall and knocked on it. A dull thud was his answer. He pulled back the curtains. The windows had large dark cushions protecting them. From the street, it would look as if they were drapes.

"The man had a lot to hide." Partlan looked around the room. "Who knows how many children he brought in and out of this house, or how long he kept them here. He could not risk his neighbors finding out about his activities."

Selena fought back her nausea. David Hendry had been twisted. To buy and sell children was horrible. Worse, he had been living in a normal neighborhood and looked like an average person. Who would have guessed the horribly diseased person he really was. Her mind shied away from the atrocities that the man might have committed, and the fact that his house had hid them all.

Malac called from the next room. "I have logged onto his computer, but there is only private photos and games on it. There is not even business correspondence."

"It will be hidden amongst pictures or other files." Catal left Selena and went to Malac.

Selena stood in the center of the room and forced her gaze away from David Hendry's body. Soon they would have what they needed and could leave this horrible place. She crossed her arms and rubbed them. A shiver of cold raced up her spine.

Ranon entered the room from the basement area. "I have searched the house. There is no one else here."

"Good." Partlan put his gun away in his waistband.

"There were a number of locked rooms in the basement. I went through them all."

"That must have been where they kept the children before he arranged for them to be transported." Selena's voice was a whisper.

She looked toward David Hendry's body. It was just as well he was dead. A monster like him didn't deserve to live. She fought back nausea when she considered all of the lives he'd ruined. Death was too easy for him. She straightened her shoulders. There was no reason to dwell on this. She needed to focus and find strength so that Tarrin and Gates could be found.

"I've found something." Catal's voice rose from the other room. "It's not much, but it seems to be a snippet of an email."

"Who is it to?" Partlan started out of the room.

"There is only one word. Diamond."

Selena went to stand beside Catal. He reached an arm around her waist and brought her closer. A sense of hope and love filled her. She leaned against him. Every muscle in her body relaxed as a warm heat suffused her.

"The truck must have the word Diamond in it." Partlan leaned down to look at the monitor. "Search the internet for trucking companies with that name."

Catal's fingers flew over the keyboard. "There is a Diamond Freezer Haulage listed for California. It's a start. We'll ask at the truck stop."

Partlan nodded. "We are wasting time here. Bring the laptop. We will check it out more fully on the road."

Malac packed up the computer and started out of the house. Catal led her past the living room and out the rear door. The night was cool, and except for the occasional car horn, it was quiet. The shrubbery around the house hid their presence. They left the neighborhood without passing another vehicle.

The drive to the truck stop took about thirty minutes. The whole time she sat beside Catal and let him hold her close. His body warmth slowly penetrated the chill that surrounded her. Soon they would have a lead to the boys. She focused on that thought.

When they reached the Castaic truck stop, they pulled into a large parking area. They slowed the van down and went up and down the long lines of parked trucks. She fought the urge to scream in frustration when they had finished perusing all of the transports. None of them had the word Diamond on it. Her hands clenched tight in her lap. Catal placed his over hers and a wave of peace descended on her. Her tension eased.

Hope filled her.

She looked up into his eyes and was mesmerized by the calm strength she saw there. He would never let her down. He would always be there for her. With a sigh she buried her face into his chest, letting the stroking of his hand on her back soothe her fears.

The boys would be found alive.

Firbin stopped the van with a screech of the brakes. "I recognize that trucker. His name is George. We met him when I was traveling with Ardal after we crashed on this planet. We were being pursued by a biker gang called the FD Warriors."

"Will he help?"

"He helped us with the bikers." Firbin opened his door. "I am certain he will again."

Firbin jumped out of the van. Partlan and Breanon followed. They were gone several minutes, which seemed more like hours. Selena stayed where she was, letting Catal's calm flow through her.

"We will have the boys soon."

"I know." Selena looked up into Catal's eyes. "Tarrin is still alive. I know it."

"I haven't been able to contact him." Catal's voice was pained. "He may not be able to connect, but we will find him."

"I trust you." Selena stretched up and kissed him. "I know now that you have never failed me."

Catal's gazed at her with an intensity that burned through to her soul. "I would die before I let any harm come to you or Tarrin."

The opening of the front door broke the spell. The others jumped into the vehicle.

"The truck went north. It had the words Diamond Freezer Haulage on its side." Firbin shifted the van into gear and was back on the highway within seconds. "It only left about fifteen minutes ago. I should have no trouble catching it."

Selena heaved a sigh.

Soon she would have Tarrin in her arms.

The van swayed and bounced as Firbin sped down the highway. Catal kept her close. She could feel the pounding of his heart against her ear. It was steady and sure. Almost an hour passed before Catal shifted in the seat. The van was slowing down.

"There it is." Firbin put the brakes on.

He swung the vehicle into a rest area and pulled up beside a semi with the words Diamond Freezer Haulage. The area was dark. The only illumination was from the truck's headlights. Selena eased away from Catal, who was checking the magazine of his pistol. All the men were arming themselves for a battle. A shiver went through her. What if one of the boys was shot by mistake.

"We wouldn't do that." Catal's low voice brushed past her ear. "We will secure them first."

"Promise?"

"Always." Catal pulled her close and let his lips brush against hers.

"I just want our son back alive."

"As do I." Catal squeezed her tight before releasing her and moving toward the van's rear door. "You stay here with Firbin."

He opened the door and jumped down with the rest of the men. She rubbed her arms with her hands to keep the chill of fear at bay. She felt useless, but it was safer for her to stay here. Catal and the others didn't need her interference. Heaving a sigh, she leaned her head against the metal side of the van and waited. Soon Tarrin would be in her arms.

She was filled with contentment until the loud retort of a gun ripped through the air and her heart.

Chapter 16

Darkness surrounded and protected Catal.

The scent of diesel, from the running truck, filled his nostrils as he eased his way around the rear of the transport and moved to the cab. A man was visible within the circle of the semi's headlights. His back was toward him and he was walking in the direction of the restrooms. There was only one other vehicle in the parking lot and it was leaving. It would be easier to ambush the truck driver before he got to the building.

Partlan motioned for him to follow their quarry.

Catal gripped his gun.

Edging away from the side of the transport, he slowed his breathing. All of his focus was on the driver. His son was somewhere inside the truck, but he had to be certain. His concentration and determination increased with each step he took. He needed information from the driver. That man held the key to his son's freedom and he intended to get it.

The man he followed was short and wide. He walked with a limp and his body looked as if it were permanently bent at the shoulders. The running engine of the truck masked Catal's footsteps. He slipped up beside the driver and nodded. The man's eyes widened in surprise. Before he could react, Catal grabbed him around the neck and covered his mouth with his hand. He dragged him off the paved path and into the bushes behind the building.

Ranon and Malac joined them.

"Where are they?" Catal's voice was a growl as he eased his hand away from the man's mouth.

"Look man, I don't carry money with me." The driver's voice shook.

"We want the boys." Catal pushed his captive against the side of the building and shoved his gun under his jaw. "We know you made arrangements to pick them up in Castaic. Are they in your cab, or the trailer?"

"I didn't pick up anything in Castaic." The man's hand shook as he lifted his keys. "You can check the truck out, but all I'm carrying is frozen food."

Catal took the keys and threw them at Ranon.

Soon the boys would be free.

He pushed back a sense of elation. He still had to deal with the driver. He turned to Malac and signaled him to hold the man while he went to follow Ranon. He wanted to be present when his son was found. Ranon moved to exchange places with Catal.

Catal's arms were away from the man for a mere second, but it was enough for the driver to free one hand. In less time than it took for a heartbeat, he had reached behind his back and pulled a gun. His finger was on the trigger just as Catal grabbed his arm and pushed it up.

The shot echoed through the night.

Catal squeezed the man's hand and banged it against the wooden side of the building until he dropped the pistol. Ranon picked it up and shoved it into his waistband.

"An innocent man wouldn't have tried to kill us." Catal strengthened his grip on the man's throat. "You must know we have no choice but to kill you for what you've done to the boys."

"I've told you there are no boys." The driver's voice was a hoarse squeak. "I don't have a clue as to what you're talking about."

"The two boys that were abducted in Los Angeles a week ago. They were seen going into your truck." Catal tightened his hands. "Kidnapping is bad enough, but lying shows you've no honor at all. Do you have any idea what was intended for the boys?"

The driver shook his head. His fear was a palatable entity. The man had done harm to children. He could not be left alive. He would only continue along the same path and many more innocent children would be hurt. There was only one option left to a Hunter.

The man must die.

Catal inhaled and lifted the man by his neck. He eyes didn't waver from the terror in the other's gaze. At least he would make his end swift and painless, which was more consideration than had been given to the boys.

"Wait." Partlan's voice rang out.

Catal eased the man to the ground. He continued to hold him by the neck, but there was no pressure in his grip. "What have you found?"

Partlan halted beside him. "The boys are not in the truck."

Catal's heart stopped for second. He turned back to the driver. "What did you do with them?"

"I told you, I don't have anything but frozen food onboard."

"You were seen leaving Castaic. We also know the boys were being held hostage on a Diamond Freezer truck." Partlan's tone was harsh.

"Do you know how big the company is?" The man's eyes shifted between him and Partlan. "There is more than one Diamond Freezer truck. As a matter of fact, I followed another Diamond truck out of Castaic."

"Where is that truck now?" Catal forced his voice to remain steady.

The man shrugged. "He turned off toward Bakersfield."

"Did you know him?"

"Only to look at. We drive for the same company, but our routes are different. I go up along the coast and he takes the interior."

"What do you know about his sideline of transporting children?" Catal raised an eyebrow.

"It's the first time I've heard anything about it." The man's voice cracked. "Hey, I've got three kids of my own. I would never keep quiet about something like that."

Catal eased his hand away from the man's neck. There was no doubting the sincerity in the man's voice. Frustration and anger battled inside of him. He took a deep breath and steadied his heartbeat. To have been so close to finding the boys and then to be disappointed was almost more than he could stand.

"What am I going to tell Selena?" Catal pushed back his anguish.

"The truth." Partlan's voice was firm. "We do not give up."

Catal nodded and took a step back from the driver. "Our information was wrong. I apologize for frightening you."

The man rubbed his neck. "No worries, man. I'm sorry I tried to shoot you, but you guys scared me. Are you sure that it was a Diamond truck the kids were put on? It just doesn't seem possible."

"Our information is correct." Partlan spoke in a quiet voice. "We have no intention of hurting the innocent. All we want is to find the boys before harm is done to them."

"I understand." The driver moved away from the wall. "I wish I could help more."

"You've told us what you know." Catal sighed. "We will find the other truck."

The driver gave him a look of unease. "Can I go now?"

"Yes." Catal moved so the man could walk away.

Catal crossed his arms and watched as the guy went back to his truck. No one could have guessed that two identical trucks would be leaving Castaic at the same time. Worse, they were both going in the same direction. It was a hard blow.

The sooner they were back on the road chasing the second truck, the better. The man had a huge start on them, and they would have to make up for lost time. They also had to consider where he was going to drop the boys off. Finding them now was going to be difficult.

When he reached the van, Selena was already outside. Her eyes were wide and her hands were clutched together at her heart. Catal gathered her close. All he could do was send her love and hope. Within seconds, he felt her body relax against him. Only then did he ease away and look at her.

"The boys aren't here."

"What was the gun shot I heard? Was anyone hurt?"

Catal shook his head. "The driver was trying to protect himself. I forced his hand into the air."

Selena's lowered lip trembled. "Now what?"

"We know there was a second truck. It turned off toward Bakersfield."

"That was miles ago."

"True." Catal touched his forehead to hers. "We will find the boys."

Selena looked up at him, her eyes filled with tears. "I'm frightened."

"I won't give up until Tarrin is back with you."

"But will it be soon enough?" Selena's voice broke. "The damage that could happen to them is more than physical. They're just young boys. How do they recover from this?"

"Tarrin is strong. He is a Hunter."

"But I've raised him, not you."

Catal grinned. "You're the toughest woman I know. You are my pair bond, which means you understand the ways of a Hunter, even if you don't realize it."

"You're trying to make me feel better. I appreciate that. The only thing that will help is to have my son in my arms and know he is safe."

Catal's chest tightened. Tarrin was lucky to have known a mother's love. It was much more than he'd ever had as a child. He pulled Selena close. To have her love was more than he deserved. He was blessed. Selena trusted him to find Tarrin and he wasn't going to disappoint her. He wouldn't stop until his son was found. It was a vow and a promise that went deeper than his obedience to the Sacred Code.

"You've said that you can sense Tarrin. Is that still possible?"

Selena moved back from his chest. "Yes, but it's getting weaker."

"I can't contact him, no matter what I try." Catal held Selena at arm's length and looked down at her. "I need you to do something for me."

"Anything."

"Does Tarrin know I am his father?"

"Not exactly." Selena glanced away for a second. "I've only told him his father was a soldier."

"Would he trust me, even though I am a stranger?"

Selena bit her lip. "I never told him anything negative about you, if that's what you're asking. Even though I felt betrayed, I couldn't let him believe that the part of him that came from his father was less than perfect."

Catal closed his eyes briefly. Selena had honor. "Could you try and send him a message that his father is trying to contact him?"

"I can't speak to him telepathically."

"But he can sense you?"

"I believe so." Selena rubbed her arms. "Do you think that if he is expecting you then you'll be able to communicate?"

"It's possible." Catal put an arm around her shoulder and led her back to the van. "Up to now he has only known you. He doesn't understand about communicating through mind connection. If you ease his fears about what to expect, he might be more open to me."

The other men were already in the van. Catal helped Selena in and seated her across from him in the rear. She seemed to sag against the metal side of the van, but within a few seconds, she straightened up. She closed her eyes. He knew Selena was sending their son positive energy and hope.

He turned to Partlan. "Selena is going to try and connect with Tarrin. Perhaps he will be more open to our communications afterwards."

"It will help. I know it was a long time ago for you, but remember your first connection when you were little more than a babe." Partlan shut the door and held onto the back of the driver's seat. "Tarrin will feel the same way as you did."

"It was a shock, I recall that much."

"And you were surrounded by your brothers and clan members." Partlan sat beside him. "Firbin is going to take us back to the turnoff. He is a fast driver, but we have lost a lot of time."

Catal nodded. "After Selena is finished, I will try and make contact with Tarrin again. Any information he can send us will help."

For the next ten minutes, they drove in silence. Firbin pushed the van to its limits as they retraced the miles. They were on the lookout for a cross road to take them to Bakersfield. If they were lucky, the truck wouldn't have reached Bakersfield. Their best chance of spotting the vehicle was in an isolated area, where it would stand out.

Catal had his eyes glued to the outside, scanning every bit of highway and side road they passed when Selena touched his hand. A jolt of heat seared him. He looked at her face and noticed a lessening of the tension.

"Have you connected with him?"

She smiled. "Yes."

"He is alive. That is good."

"I've sent him thoughts about you. I don't know if he understands my message, but I sent it to him."

"He will sense that you are near." Catal took her hand and squeezed it. "Let me try now."

She nodded and moved back into her seat. "I pray you'll be able to connect with him."

Catal crossed his arms and leaned back. The other warriors in the van were busy checking their weapons. They understood, like Partlan, how difficult the first connection could be. They were giving him privacy, so he could concentrate. Catal took a deep breath and focused.

He'd been about three when he'd first heard the voices of his fellow Hunters. It had meant the end of his childhood and the beginning of his training as a warrior. The most disconcerting thing was that it had been so unexpected and painful for the first couple of connections. After that, it had become second nature, but he could still remember the fear and doubt the first time he'd heard his mentor speak to him with thoughts.

It was a secret that only Hunters shared. Not even their teachers, who were Kaladin, knew of the mind connection. Their telepathic ability was probably the result of centuries of genetic modifications and manipulation. Some of their legends said that when time began they had been able to connect to others through their mind, but the ability had been lost. Necessity and survival had forced their breed to remember how to speak to each other without words.

Catal didn't care why he could connect, he just knew that it had saved his life many times. It also made them unique. No matter how strongly the Kaladin held control over their lives and actions, there was still a part of them that was private and secret. No one outside their brotherhood knew about it except their mates, and until they had come to Earth, they hadn't had mates.

Tarrin might feel a connection with his mother, but he wouldn't understand the voice that would be pushing to be heard inside his mind. And that was exactly what Catal had to do. He had to force Tarrin to hear him and respond. It was the difference between life and death.

He sent out wave after wave of mind connection. His words were simple. *"Tarrin it is Catal, your father. I am here to help you."*

He sent the same message time and again. Along with words, he sent love and hope. He knew from his first connection that it sometimes took days for the voices to be heard. He fervently prayed that wouldn't be the case. They didn't have the luxury of time.

The van had turned off toward Bakersfield when Catal felt a glimmer of a response. It was hesitant and a faint whisper in his mind, but he knew it was Tarrin.

"Are you real?"

"Yes." Catal let his mind connect fully. *"You mother sent for me. My brothers and I have come to rescue you and Gates."*

Catal knew that the more specific he was with names, the more real it would seem to Tarrin. The first mind connect was always met with doubt and concern, even for a young child. Tarrin was older than most for his first connection, so the doubts would be greater.

"How can you help us?" This time Tarrin's voice was stronger.

"*I am a warrior. I've been trained since I was younger than you to deal with the situation you are in, but I need your cooperation.*"

"*What can I do?*"

"*We know which road the truck holding you, is driving on. Has it made any stops? Have you been let out?*"

"*It stopped once for about ten minutes.*" Tarrin's voice faded away for a second and then came back stronger. "*We didn't get out, but the driver did. I heard his door slam.*"

"*Has the truck made any turns?*"

"*Yes. The truck swayed to the right for a bit and then a few minutes after that we stopped.*"

"*Did he talk to anyone?*"

"*I didn't hear voices.*"

"*How long ago was the stop?*"

"*Gates and I counted to over one thousand before the truck started moving. Right now Gates is counting to six hundred.*"

"*Good.*" A surge of pride went through Catal. If they counted at a steady pace that meant at least fifteen minutes had passed. "*I'm going to use your counting to figure out where you are. What I need you to do is tell me when you stop again. Just shout out my name and focus. I will hear you.*"

"*Okay.*" There was a slight pause. "*You won't leave Gates and I alone, will you?*"

"*We will be there to rescue you.*" Catal's voice hardened. "*These men will pay the price for taking you, so don't be frightened when we arrive.*"

"*I'll tell Gates.*"

"*Be strong.*" Catal broke the connection and turned to Partlan. "They turned right and then stopped for about fifteen minutes. Since then they've driven about ten minutes. Is there a rest area?"

Partlan pulled a mapping device toward him and started to punch in numbers. He frowned and shook his head. "No. I am going to calculate the approximate distance they traveled in the time since they left Castaic."

Catal reached over and clasped Selena's hands. "We will find them. Tarrin is able to mind connect, so that will make this easier."

Selena gave him a weak smile. "Thank you. Knowing that you've been able to speak with him, gives me hope."

"Firbin we are on the correct road. It will lead to the freeway." Partlan looked up from the mapping system. "I think the most likely place the driver turned was onto a road going east. It's a trucking route that bypasses Bakersfield."

Firbin nodded. "I should be there in a couple of minutes."

Firbin increased their speed. They might have lost time following the wrong truck, but they could catch up. Going cross country between the two highways would save time. Within a few minutes, they had reached the junction with the Golden State Highway. Now all they needed was to find the truck.

"Keep along this road." Partlan looked up from his calculations. "This is the most likely route."

Just then Catal heard Tarrin's voice in his head. *"We're slowing down."*

"Is it stopping?" Catal held his breath. They still hadn't found the truck. If they stopped now, they might be too late to rescue the boys.

"Yes." Tarrin's voice came stronger. *"I can hear honking and other traffic. Now the truck is starting to drive again."*

"Good." Catal forced his muscles to relax. There was still hope. *"Is there anything different about how the truck is driving?"*

"It is moving slower."

Catal turned to Partlan. "They have slowed down and the truck made a stop, and then started."

Partlan tapped the map. "We are on the right road. It runs through a built up area and that would mean stoplights."

A few minutes later Tarrin connected again.

"The truck has stopped."

"It is important you give us every detail now."

Tarrin was silent for a few seconds. *"We are turning right."*

Catal let out the breath he'd been holding. They weren't at their final destination. That was good. They were close behind, but the truck wasn't in sight yet. The longer the driver kept moving, the better chance they had of catching them.

"I need you to start counting so we know when you stop or turn again."

"They've turned right." Catal looked at Partlan. "Tarrin is going to keep time by counting so we'll know where they turn again."

"I think they are going south." Partlan looked up from the map. "We are close behind. A few more minutes and we should have them in sight."

A sob from Selena had Catal moving beside her. He pulled her close and brought her head to his chest. He let his hand smooth over her hair. Her suffering was his. He felt it to the very core of his being. The sound of her steady breathing soothed him.

"We are close." His voice was a soft whisper. "We will have them soon."

"*We turned left.*" Tarrin's voice sounded in his head. "*I only had to count to three hundred.*"

"*I'll put that into our computer,*" Catal answered.

"They've turned left. It took about five minutes."

"They're going north to Caliente." Partlan leaned toward Firbin and showed him the map. "Follow the same route. He should be in sight soon."

"*I can hear a train whistle.*" Tarrin's voice sounded more like a whisper. "*We're slowing down again.*"

"They're near a train."

Partlan nodded. "Definitely Caliente."

Firbin came to a stop and then turned right. A few minutes later he turned left. They were close now. The road was straight for a bit and Firbin sped along until they started to hit curves and steep hills. They slowed and then sped up again. They came into a small town, which was Caliente. Now all of them were looking outside for sight of the truck. It should still be travelling on the road according to Tarrin.

Suddenly, Firbin put the brakes on.

The red running lights of the rear of a transport truck were visible in front of them.

They went around a curve and the van's headlights illuminated the word Diamond. The truck that held the boys, was in front of them.

Chapter 17

"Turn our lights off." Partlan's tone was tense.

"I have." Firbin's voice was low.

"Good." Partlan squatted down beside Firbin. "We do not want him to know we are following."

The mood in the van became somber. Always ready for battle, now they had increased their concentration tenfold. As long as the driver of the truck was unaware of their presence, they should be able to follow him to his lair.

Catal rubbed Selena's arm and kept his eyes glued on the red taillights of the semi. It was a quarter of a mile ahead of them. The lights brightened and Firbin eased the van to a stop. The truck turned right and they followed.

"*We just turned.*" Tarrin's voice echoed in Catal's head.

"*I know.*" Catal kept his thoughts calm. "*We are directly behind you.*"

"*Are you going to stop him now?*"

"*No. I need for you to be brave.*" Catal knew that Tarrin wouldn't understand, because he hadn't had any training, but they had to let the truck get to its destination. It was the safest way to rescue the boys. "*When the truck stops, we will be there to free you.*"

There was a few moments of silence and then he heard Tarrin's voice. "*You want to make sure he won't get away.*"

"*We can't risk losing you. When he stops we'll have the advantage.*"

"*I'll let Gates know that there is nothing to be afraid of.*"

After that there was silence. Catal watched the vehicle weave and turn on the winding road. Sparse plantings of trees along the shoulders could be seen from the glare of the truck's headlights, but no houses. They were definitely going to an isolated area.

They slowed after twenty minutes. Catal exhaled, stretched his neck from side to side, and eased his heart rate as he prepared for battle. He gave Selena's hand a reassuring squeeze before moving away. He picked up two pistols and secured them in his jean's waistband. Partlan handed him a rifle and he checked the ammunition before resting it across his knees. He was as ready as possible.

The truck went down a gravel laneway. There was a marker at the road stating it was private property. The semi bounced up and down, and side to side, in front of them. It would not be comfortable for the boys inside the truck. They had to be near the location for the exchange. There was no other reason for a large tractor trailer to travel such a rutted and narrow laneway. Soon the boys would be freed. Then he would exact justice on those who were responsible for this crime.

Firbin parked at the edge of the paved road.

Everyone jumped out of the vehicle.

Selena tried to leave, but Catal held her back. "It's not safe for you to come with us."

"I can shoot. My brother insisted I learn."

Catal clenched his jaw. "That's not the problem, I don't want you hurt. It's a dangerous situation."

"I'll be careful." Selena's voice was determined. "I won't be left behind a second time, especially when I know that my son is definitely on that truck."

Catal looked over at Partlan. He knew the others still believed that women were to be obeyed, yet his time on Earth had shown him that they weren't used to commanding on this planet. Partlan's expression gave nothing away.

Catal gazed at Selena for several seconds and then nodded. She was his pair bond. He couldn't refuse her. There was nothing he could say to stop her either. She had always been stubborn. Once she'd made a decision, nothing would deter her from it. That's how she'd been able to block him for so many years. All he could do was ensure she remained safe.

He handed her a pistol.

"Stay behind me."

The transport truck they had been following had continued for several hundred yards on a driveway that circled a large building that was hidden beneath a stand of pine trees. The place would be invisible from the road and the air. There were at least ten vehicles parked along the edge of the drive, amongst the trees. The semi had stopped, and was facing the road, when they reached the building. It was still running. It looked as if the driver didn't plan to stay long.

Partlan motioned Firbin and Malac to the vehicle. Breanon moved off to the side and lay beside a large pine, assault rifle aimed and ready. Ranon and Partlan moved to the side door of the building. Catal and Selena went to the front.

Partlan signaled for Firbin and Malac to enter the truck. The door was unlocked. The first thing they did was shut the vehicle off. A few seconds later, they climbed down from the cab and shook their head.

The boys weren't there.

They took the keys and went to the rear of the semi. It wouldn't take the people inside the building long to realize the truck had stopped running. Time was important. The wind caught the back door of the trailer and sent it slamming against the side of the truck.

A chill of warning raced up Catal's spine.

He pulled Selena close behind him, and readied for battle. The occupants of the hideaway had to have heard the noise. They now knew they weren't alone. They'd prepare themselves for a fight. They didn't have long to wait before someone inside made a move.

The front door edged open a crack.

The barrel of a rifle poked through.

Catal stood behind the door and waited until it opened wider. Two hands and a head followed the gun. Catal's eyes narrowed and his breathing slowed. Selena's unease surrounded him, but he blocked it. He had to focus all of his attention on his next move.

"*Go.*" Partlan gave the command.

Catal slammed the door against the unseen opponent. A yelp of surprise echoed in the still night air. Catal opened the door and slammed it again before he pulled the man out of the opening and threw him onto the ground.

The man raised his gun to fire.

Catal shot him between the eyes.

Footsteps and yelling could be heard from inside the building. They didn't wait to see who would come out next. Partlan and Ranon stormed the side door at the same time Catal and Selena went in the front. Chaos was everywhere as men scattered in all directions. There had to be at least twelve men ranging in age from mid-twenties to their sixties. A few raised their guns to fire at them and they were met with a bullet.

Catal shot to kill anyone who raised a weapon in his direction. Partlan and Ranon did the same from the side entrance. They moved through the building killing all those who got in their way, or tried to escape. They rounded up all the men who were left alive into the center of the large hall. Six remained standing and they threw their weapons to the ground.

The shooting came to an abrupt end.

"Who are you?" A man in a black suit spoke. He was in his sixties and stood with his hands over his head. "This is a private club."

"One that is dealing in kidnapping." Partlan motioned for Ranon to gather the guns. "Where are the children?"

"This is a men's club. No children are allowed." The man gave a soft laugh. "You'll have to find another group to terrorize."

"I think not." Catal moved forward. "We know the truck outside was carrying two boys that were kidnapped from their home."

"The truck has nothing to do with us." The man shrugged. "You've killed the driver, so I doubt you'll be able to ask him any questions."

Firbin and Malac came into the building and shook their heads. "It was empty."

"That means you've hid them here." Selena's voice rang out behind Catal. "Tarrin, tell me where you are?"

There was no answer.

"You can yell all you want, but there's no one here." The man grinned. "I'm a judge with very influential friends. Why don't you leave while you have a chance?"

For a second Catal wondered if they'd barged in on the wrong building, but then he heard a faint whisper in his head.

"*We're in the dark.*" Tarrin's voice held fear.

"*Is there someone guarding you?*"

"*Yes. He has a gun that has a red light that he keeps moving over all of us. He told us to be quiet or he'd kill us.*"

"They're in a hidden room with at least one guard." Catal looked back at Selena. "We will find them."

Selena nodded. "I'll keep them covered while you search."

The judge took a step forward. "You don't think one little lady can hold all of us?"

Selena fired her pistol.

The bullet hit an inch away from the man's foot.

"I hit where I aim. You have no idea how angry a mother can be when her children have been hurt." Selena's voice held suppressed fury. "I'm seconds away from forgetting I abhor violence."

The man stepped back.

"Firbin help Selena guard these people." Partlan lowered his arm. "The rest of us will search."

Catal looked at Selena to be certain she was comfortable holding the men at gunpoint. She seemed to sense his question and nodded. He went with Partlan. They began by checking out all of the doors that opened into the main building. They were mainly for storage. Two rooms had camera equipment and a studio set up. One was a computer room.

All were empty.

Malac examined the walls by knocking on them. They were solid pine. There were no secret passageways or doors.

"*See if Tarrin remembers anything about the room?*" Partlan looked at Catal.

Catal nodded. "*Tarrin how did you get into the hiding place?*"

"*Our eyes were covered.*" There was a pause. "*We had to crouch and go down a couple of stairs. When they took the blindfolds off it was dark.*"

"*It's underground.*" Catal sent the message to the rest of the unit.

Ranon and Malac began to kick the floor looking for hollow sounds. Catal searched for any obvious breaks in the floorboards. He moved toward the rear of the building. There was a cloakroom and a ten foot bar there. The cloakroom was empty. The bar had dark wooden shelves set up against a mirror backdrop. There were liquor bottles and glasses of all sizes. Under the bar top, there were more bottles. Catal's eyes scanned the oak floor and that's when he saw it.

The floor was covered with sand and dirt except a two foot by two foot area.

The right size for a trap door.

"Look, you boys should be getting out of here before the police arrive." The judge took a step forward.

"I doubt that." Firbin's voice was full of disgust. "The last thing you would want is for the police to take a close look at your men's club."

Catal eased out of the bar area. There was at least one man down there with a gun pointed at the children. He couldn't risk the man shooting one of the boys before they had a chance to kill the guard. It would take a coordinated effort to get them out alive.

"Men is the last word I'd use to describe you." Catal nodded to Partlan. "Take one more move and you're dead."

"*There's a trapdoor behind the bar, but the boys are being held by someone with a laser sight gun.*"

"Then Tarrin will guide us." Partlan's voice was emotionless. "*Can he assist with the rescue?*"

Catal reached out to Tarrin. "*We know where you are, but you will have to help. Are you up to that?*"

"Yes." Tarrin's voice was determined. "*What do I have to do?*"

"*When I say go, I need you to rush the man holding you and push his arm and gun up away from the others. We will do the rest.*"

"Ranon and Malac help guard the captives." Partlan gave the commands in a harsh voice. "If anyone moves or speaks, kill them."

When Ranon and Malac had taken up their positions Partlan joined Catal behind the bar. They stood on each side of the trapdoor and readied their weapons. Catal took a deep breath. He pulled out his knife and slid it into the gap between the door and the floor. He glanced up at Partlan, who aimed his rifle at the opening. One nod and Catal's mind reached out for Tarrin.

"*Go.*"

He flipped the trapdoor open as a gun fired.

The bullet streaked past his ear.

In the next second, he grabbed his assailant by the neck and pulled him out of the hole. He snapped the man's neck with one swift movement. He threw the body over the bar and turned back just as Partlan kicked the pistol out of the hand of a second man.

The man reached to grab one of the boys as a hostage.

Partlan snatched the boy away from harm.

Catal's arm locked around the man's throat. He squeezed and twisted, breaking the second man's neck. That's when the captives in the center of the building started to move. Gunshots rang throughout the air. When everything had settled down, another two men were dead. The rest had stayed in place.

Catal dragged the man he had killed out of the bar area. The boy that Partlan was holding, watched. His eyes were wide, but there was no fear in them, only acceptance. When the area was clear of bodies, Catal reached into the hole and pulled out the children. In total, there were four boys and two girls. The children stayed huddled together. They kept their eyes lowered and it wasn't until Selena's spoke that they looked up.

"Is Tarrin alive?"

The boy Partlan was holding turned his head. "Mom?"

Catal's heart constricted as he watched Tarrin run to Selena. This was his son. He had kept his promise to Selena and delivered him unharmed.

"Go to them. We will take care of the other children. I will keep them in the cloak room so they do not have to see their captors again." Partlan's voice was low.

Catal looked over at the other warrior. His face was expressionless, but his eyes held understanding and awe. Never before had a Hunter had a child. Centuries of breeding and training to be warriors was now at variance with the wonder of fatherhood. Love and pride, emotions that were foreign and unsettling, stirred deep within him.

He took a step toward them.

Selena turned at his approach and held her arms out to him. Within seconds, he was cocooned within the love and peace of holding her and his son. Tears of joy flowed from Selena's eyes. She looked up at him and smiled.

"Thank you for giving me my son back."

Catal didn't trust his voice. Instead, he nodded and led them to the door. He couldn't relax until he knew they were away from this place. Only then would he feel that they were safe and that his mission had been accomplished. There was still the mess of dealing with the dead and captives.

There was also the question of the other children they had found. They had homes and parents who were worried about their whereabouts. These were problems that had to be resolved before he could take Selena and Tarrin home. Just the thought of leaving them sent a piercing stab of pain to his heart. He had only just found them. To lose them was unthinkable, but he had no other choice. It was Selena's decision. If she wanted him to stay away, then he must honor her wishes.

They reached the front door. Behind them was the commotion of the captives being moved to the far wall, as the children came out from behind the bar area. He opened the door and waited until Selena and Tarrin had left, before turning back to the room. Partlan and Ranon were with the children. Firbin held the others at gunpoint while Malac was slipping plastic handcuffs on them.

Catal left the building and caught up with Selena and Tarrin. "Everything is under control. We need to get you to the van."

"What about Gates." Tarrin spoke for the first time. "He's afraid and I promised to take care of him."

"I forgot completely." Selena's voice held regret as she looked up at Catal. "Could you get him?"

Catal nodded. He turned to go back. A yell from inside the building had him reaching for the pistol in his jean's waistband. Before he had a chance to aim his weapon, a figure appeared at the door. It was the judge.

He had a gun in his hands and he was pointing it straight at them. Catal pushed Selena and Tarrin behind him just as the man fired. Catal raised his gun, but before he could fire, another shot rang out. Breanon's aim was true. The judge dropped dead.

Catal stumbled as a searing pain in his arm forced him back a step. He put his hand up to his arm to stop the flow of blood that gushed from the wound.

He'd been shot.

Chapter 18

Catal lurched against her.

Selena looked up at his face. Her heart stopped when she saw his grimace of pain. He'd been hurt. She grabbed him before he could turn away, her hands patted at his body in a frantic effort to find the wound. She gripped his arm and he groaned.

"How bad is it?"

"A mere scratch." Catal struggled to stand straight. "I've had worse."

"Not when you've been with me." Selena forced the panic out of her voice. "Let me see it."

"Not here." Catal straightened up and took her arm. He continued to walk her and Tarrin back to the road. "We need to get you two into the van. I'll come back and get Gates."

"You can't expect me to let you go without stopping the bleeding?"

"Yes you can." Catal's voice was determined. He stopped when they reached the parked van and opened the rear door. He lifted his son into the vehicle, then started to leave.

"Tarrin needs you. I'm not seriously injured."

"You would never leave me alone and hurt." Selena put her hands on her hips. "I love you. The pair bond you talk about is just as strong for me."

Catal turned back to her. He raised his uninjured arm and let his fingers feather down her cheek. "Nothing is going to happen to me. The others already have everything under control."

"I have to be certain." Selena forced back a sob. "You were almost killed."

"That happens every day in my line of work."

"Not when I'm with you."

Selena grabbed his arm and ripped open his sleeve. Her fingers moved over the wound. The bullet had grazed his skin, nothing more. She sighed and reached into the van to pull out the first aid kit. A swabbing with an alcohol pad, gauze, antibiotic cream, and tape had the bleeding stopped and her heart beating at a slower rate.

He'd almost died trying to protect her and Tarrin. How dare he believe that she wouldn't be worried about it? She'd be devastated if anything happened to him. The thought of it was too much to bear. She reached up and touched his face.

"I never wanted you dead, even when I thought that you had betrayed me."

He nodded. "You have truly accepted our bonding."

"I thought I had already made that clear to you." Selena stood on tip toes and brushed her lips across his. Electricity seemed to spark between them. She gaze directly into his eyes. "I love you."

A pull on her top forced her to break eye contact with Catal and look back at Tarrin.

"Is he my father?" Tarrin was looking at Catal with unblinking eyes.

Selena smiled. "Yes."

Catal put a hand on Tarrin's head. She sensed, more than heard, an unspoken communication between the two. Tarrin's eyes widened and then he pointed to the building. Catal nodded and went to get Gates.

Selena gathered Tarrin close and hugged him tight. Her son was free and unharmed. Never in the past week, had she let herself envision this moment, for fear of it not happening. Catal and his fellow Hunters had made it possible. They hadn't given up. She owed them so much.

"Did those men hurt you?"

Tarrin shook his head. "They scared me, but I had to be strong for Gates. He was crying."

"It must have been very frightening for both of you."

"Once I heard Catal's voice in my head, I was fine." Tarrin gave her a small smile. "He said that he would come for me. That's when I knew we'd be safe."

"He's a very brave man." Selena choked back a sob. "You are just like him."

"We look alike. He's big like me too."

"Yes." Selena stood. "You will be as tall as him one day."

"Will I be a warrior too?"

Tears started to form in Selena's eyes. She knew it was normal for a boy to want to be like his father, but the thought of her baby becoming a warrior, made her chest constrict with fear. She could barely stand the fact that Catal put his life on the line every day. To think that her son would do the same, was too much to bear.

"You have plenty of time before you have to make that decision." Selena pushed away from the van when she noticed Catal coming down the drive with a boy by his side. "Let's get Gates."

They ran to meet them and Selena pulled Gates into her arms. "Are you alright? Your mom and Dad were so worried about you."

"Tarrin kept me safe." Gates voice wobbled. "Is it true that you asked Tarrin's father to find us?"

"Yes." Selena stood and turned Gates to Catal. "This is Catal. He is a man of many skills, including finding lost children."

"Thank you." Gate's voice was solemn.

"It is safe to come inside now." Catal's voice was husky. "The criminals are secured and we are trying to figure out who the children are. You might be able to help with that. They seem very frightened of us."

"I can imagine." Selena's chest tightened at the thought of what these children had been put through at the hands of the men in that building. Tarrin and Gates had been kidnapped and then sold. That was probably the case for the other children.

They walked into the building. The remaining captives were sitting against the wall. Their hands were cuffed behind them and they were attached to iron rings that were secured on the walls. The dead bodies were laid out further down the hall. On the opposite side of the room there tables and chairs set up. It looked like a men's club, just like the judge claimed. Probably most of its members had no clue that it had another use.

Selena turned her eyes toward the children at the back of the building. They were in the cloak room and hovering together. Their eyes were downcast, and their bodies turned away from Ranon and Partlan who were standing guard over them. It was obvious they feared their rescuers. They were probably terrified of all adults, but she would try and help sort out their names.

"You boys stay with Catal." Selena straightened her shoulders. "Do either of you know the other children?"

"When we got here they put us in the hold with them right away." Tarrin spoke in a matter of fact tone. "The truck driver thought he'd heard a vehicle behind him, and when he told the others, they herded us together. That's when they put blindfolds on us and told us to be quiet."

Selena nodded and went to the children. She squatted down in front of the group and held out her hand. She wasn't a trained counselor and that's what these children needed. She was a mother and worked as a nanny, though. She knew that sometimes the simplest and most honest approach was the best way to begin.

"I'm Selena."

She waited for a response, but none of the children turned to her. She tried again. She motioned to Tarrin to join her. She put her arm around her son. "This boy is my son. He and his friend were kidnapped almost a week ago."

The children glanced over their shoulders for a second.

"We're here to help you find your families."

One of the taller boys looked at her directly. "I haven't seen my mother for days. Those men said that she was dead."

Selena's fought back her tears. "They only said that so you wouldn't try and run away. What's your name?"

"Samuel."

"Where do you live?"

"Seattle."

"Good." Selena touched his hand. "If you know your address we will get you back to your mother as soon as possible. That's what we want to do for all of you."

One by one the children began to talk. They had all arrived at the building that day. They were traumatized, and would require counselling for the ordeal they had suffered. Partlan and Ranon took down the information each child provided and then grouped the names together by location. When this had been done, the children went over to where Tarrin and Gates were and sat on the floor. They stayed in the cloakroom away from their captors.

Catal came over to Selena when she'd finished with the last child. "It should be easier to get them home now. Thank you."

"I find it difficult to understand how this could happen. It would never have been tolerated on Cygnus." Partlan's voice was severe.

"I warned you that humans were different." Catal's voice was weary. "There are many atrocities that occur on this planet that would never be allowed elsewhere in the universe."

"We don't allow it here." Selena's voice was defensive. "These men will be prosecuted."

"They will be given short sentences. The only reason we are leaving any of them alive is so the FBI can question them. They may be able to get information from them about other abducted and missing children." Catal's tone was scornful. "It would be better if we could kill them now. At least honor would be satisfied."

"Perhaps, but violence is not the solution." Selena understood how Catal felt, but she still had to hope that there was a better way. One in which a person saw how wrong their actions were.

"They will be sent to prison for a short time, but the damage they've done to the children will last them a lifetime." Catal crossed his arms.

"True." Selena sighed. "It isn't perfect, but at least these children will go home to their families. There has been some justice done today."

Ranon handed Partlan a computer. "There is a lot of information on this system that might help keep these men and others like them in jail for a long time."

Partlan put the computer on the bar so that everyone could look. He started scanning through files. "They kept all of their records and transactions here. If the police act quickly enough they should be able to rescue others."

"They will have to hit all these groups at once." Catal was looking over Partlan's shoulder.

"There are papers down in the hole." Ranon looked to Partlan for direction.

"Bring them all up. We will take pictures of everything and email it to Agent Kelly." Partlan looked over at the men along the wall. "Take pictures of the captives and the bodies. See if you can get their identification."

Catal moved away from the bar. "I'll get a camera."

Selena went back over to the children and gathered Tarrin and Gates close to her on the floor. She stayed with them until the photos had been taken. The men being held were not cooperative about giving up their names, but their identification was in their wallets, so those pictures were included with the others. It took about an hour for the place to be processed and by that time the kids were starting to yawn.

Tarrin and Gates had already put their heads on her lap and were sleeping.

Catal sat beside her as he downloaded everything from the computer they'd found and emailed it to the police. He made a backup, saved it onto a memory stick, and then put the stick in his pocket.

When Selena raised an eyebrow, he shrugged. "I don't trust any human except you. This is in case the files get lost or tampered with while the police are investigating. If that happens, we will ensure that justice is done."

"I didn't realize you were so cynical."

"Humans have taught me that." Catal closed the computer. "Being careful has saved my life more than once."

Partlan joined them at that moment. "Everything is ready to go. We will leave these men here with the bodies, and contact the police when we are safely on the highway."

"I have already emailed Agent Kelly."

Partlan nodded. "She will be expecting us in Los Angeles."

"What about the other children?" Selena roused the two boys sleeping on her lap and stood. "We can't just leave them here."

"They will come with us." Partlan motioned toward the others. "There are vehicles parked outside. Firbin has found the keys on the men. We will split up."

"How many of the children need to go north?" Catal was the first to speak.

"There are two. Ranon and Malac will leave them with their families. I am going south to return Gates to his parents. Firbin and Breanon will head east with the other children."

"What about me?" Catal frowned. "Am I going with you to Beverly Hills?"

Partlan crossed his arms. "Ardal has asked you to meet him at the Blackfeet Reservation in Montana. He has some information to impart. The reservation is the safest place to gather. Niail's mate lives without electricity and contact with the outside world. That should ensure privacy."

Catal nodded. "I can head that way after Selena and Tarrin are safe."

"There is one thing I need to ascertain." Partlan turned to Selena. "Ardal, our leader would like to meet your son. Is it possible for you to go with Catal to Montana now?"

Selena felt Catal stiffen beside her. Her mind started to spin with the implications. If she and Tarrin went with Catal, they would be arriving as a family. Her heart pounded faster. Was she ready? She knew she loved him. She hadn't trusted him in the past, and that had forced them to spend years apart. Years of longing and anguish.

She'd denied him knowing his son.

She straightened her shoulders. She wasn't going to live in fear again. She loved Catal. She needed him with her always. Now wasn't the time to hesitate. She would go with him to Montana and become a part of his life. He was her mate. She couldn't bear to live without him anymore.

"Yes." Selena reached for Catal's hand. "We'll go with him."

Chapter 19

"Can we stop somewhere for the night?" Selena yawned. They had just passed through Las Vegas. "Tarrin fell asleep an hour ago and I don't think I can go on much longer."

"I want to put as much distance between us and Caliente as possible." Catal didn't take his eyes off the road.

"We've been driving for hours."

Catal glanced over at her and frowned. "It's only two in the morning."

"So it's about time we stopped for the night." Selena's voice was tired. "You can't expect to drive twenty hours straight through to Montana."

"That's exactly what I would have done. I forgot humans need rest." Catal turned off the road and pulled into the parking lot of a small two-storey hotel. "Will this do?"

All Selena cared about was stopping. They had driven without a break since taking one of the SUV's from the cabin. Catal hadn't said a word about her decision to come with him to Montana. He'd helped load the children in vehicles and then they'd left. That had been four hours ago.

Fifteen minutes later, she watched as Catal carried Tarrin into the separate bedroom of the suite they had rented for the night. It was larger than they needed, but it was the last available room. Selena threw the cellphone her brother had given her into the wastebasket. As promised, she'd contacted him and let him know that Tarrin was safe. She had also mentioned that after talking with Catal, it looked like Pablo had probably been the traitor. Now she lay across the bed. After days of worry and fear, she was exhausted. There was still one more thing to do before she could sleep.

She needed to talk with Catal.

They had to discuss where their relationship was headed.

Catal came back into the room and shut Tarrin's door. "I don't think much would wake him now."

"It's a reaction after all the terror of not knowing what was going to happen to him." Selena sat up. "I know exactly how he feels."

"Get some sleep." Catal sat in the chair by the window. "I'll keep watch."

"Is that necessary?"

He shrugged. "Force of habit more than anything else. We should be safe here. We're in a different state, and the others won't tell the authorities where we're going."

"So we can talk without interruption." Selena couldn't keep the anxiety from her voice.

What if Catal refused?

Selena didn't think she could bear that. Now that she had found him again, there was no way she would be able to leave him. He was essential for her existence. He had invaded her thoughts and her soul. To move ahead together, they had to be clear about what their expectations were.

"If that is what you want." Catal leaned forward in his chair.

Selena cleared her throat. "You haven't said a word since I agreed to come with you."

"What's there to say?" Catal's jaw tightened. "I appreciate that you are traveling with me to see Ardal. It's important that Tarrin understand his heritage. Ardal is clan Rioge, a leader. He will oversee and be responsible for Tarrin, just as he is for all Hunters on this planet."

"That's not why I came with you." Selena touched his arm. "I want to be with you."

Catal frowned. "You've said you always loved me, but you may still leave me. I will accept whatever your decision is."

"Just like that?" Selena couldn't keep the exasperation from her voice. "What about fighting for what you want?"

"I fight all the time."

"I mean do you care enough to fight for me and Tarrin." Selena threw her hands down on her lap.

"You're a woman." Catal's voice showed confusion. "You make the decisions and I must accept them. I am bonded to you for life. There will be no other woman for me, but you."

"And that means you will just let me go?"

"Never." Catal shook his head. "I want you to be my mate, but I can't force you. I obey the Sacred Code and that means I honor a woman's wishes."

Selena tilted her head. "I haven't issued you any orders."

It was suddenly clear to Selena. Despite being bonded to her, Catal would not force her to stay. She had rejected him once. She was the one who had to make him believe that she wanted him always. It was crazy. Catal had moved heaven and earth to find Tarrin, he had taken a bullet protecting them, and yet he didn't trust that she would always want him as her mate.

There was only one thing she could do.

"So you have to obey women?" Selena stood.

"Women make the decisions on Cygnus." Catal's eyes narrowed as he watched her approach.

"Well I've made a decision." Selena squatted down in front of Catal and put her hands on his knees. "I am bonded to you. I want to spend the rest of my life with you. I've decided that there is only one man for me."

Selena paused and looked directly into Catal's eyes. "I want you to marry me."

"You want me as your mate forever?" Catal's voice held awe.

"Yes." Selena stroked a finger down his hand. "I was a foolish child when we were first bonded. I had been sheltered and knew nothing about the world or how others could manipulate it."

"You know I didn't betray you." There was a catch in his voice as she bent her head and kissed his hand.

"True." Selena leaned back and smiled up at him. "I should have spoken to you about the incident. I loved you, but I didn't trust myself, or our love enough, to ask the tough questions. That's how mature people work things out. Running away only made it worse."

"At first, I thought something had happened to you." Catal's fingers twisted around hers. "I searched for you always, even after I had accepted that you didn't want me to find you. I never stopped desiring you."

"I was a foolish girl." Selena stood. "Now I am a woman. I know what I need."

Catal's eyes never left hers. "And what is that?"

"You."

Selena leaned down and placed a light kiss on Catal's lips. A gleam of light appeared in his eyes. She held her breath, waiting for his reaction. It didn't take long. Before she had taken a second breath, he had gathered her in his arms, and was carrying her to the bed.

"I hope you're certain." Catal's arms tightened around her. "I couldn't bear to lose you again."

"I have no intention of letting you go." Selena clasped her hands around his neck. "Do you know how many nights I couldn't sleep because the memory of your kisses haunted me?"

"Every waking hour, I longed to hold you again. You invaded my thoughts. I would be pleasuring you in my dreams, only to be torn from your arms by the dawn of a new day."

"Then let's not waste any time."

Catal captured her lips in a searing kiss. His tongue delved into her mouth and explored with a hunger that couldn't be denied. Selena answered him back, pulling him closer until there was no space between them. Her body burned with the desire she had suppressed.

She couldn't wait any longer.

She brought her hand down along the front of Catal's shirt and pulled it up from the bottom. "You have too many clothes on."

"So do you." Catal laid her on the bed and then joined her. "Let me help you."

One by one his fingers fumbled with the small buttons of her blouse until he had the shirt open. He pushed it aside and ran his palm over her stomach, before moving up to her breasts. His fingers feathered across the lacy front of her bra and a sharp jolt of electricity shot through her. Her body flushed with warmth and yearning.

Catal unzipped, and moved her jeans and underwear off her hips. His fingers trailed down her legs as he pulled the pants off her. Liquid heat flowed where he touched. His lips and tongue traced a path upwards. When he reached her stomach, he stopped and frowned. His finger traced over the faint white scar across her lower abdomen.

"This is new." He looked up at her. "What's it from?"

"I had Tarrin by Caesarian."

"They cut him out of you?" Catal's voice held horror.

"He was a large baby." Selena took his hand in hers. "I was too small to deliver him naturally."

"I should have been there." He shook his head. "I can't imagine how you could have gone through that alone."

"It was my decision." Selena smiled. "Can you forgive me for keeping Tarrin a secret?"

Catal's eyes widened. "There is nothing to forgive. The choice has always been yours."

"Then I chose to continue making love." She pulled him up beside her. "Now you need to get rid of your clothes."

"As you command."

Catal pulled off his shirt and then his pants. He threw them on the floor. Then he lay down beside her on the bed. His arms encircled her and pulled her close as he started to kiss her. All thoughts ceased as his hands roamed over her body, pushing and pulling the rest of her clothes off, until she was as naked as him.

She trembled with need.

Their passion burned.

Too many years had passed, and the hunger was too great, for them to take their time. All Selena wanted was to feel him deep within her. Only that would ease the ache that had been with her since the moment she had ran away from him. Even in her anger at his supposed betrayal, she had known that she would only feel whole with Catal by her side. The bond they shared was unique.

Catal's hands became more insistent. He skimmed over her back and then flitted across her breasts. A sharp jolt of desire touched her womb. Her hips moved against him in a restless invitation for more. He didn't disappoint.

His lips left hers and moved along her neck and then her breasts. His tongue flicked across one nipple sending a shudder of pleasure throughout her. A delicious tension built within. He left her breasts and moved down to her stomach. His lips caressed her abdomen, licking and soothing every inch of her scar until she was a molten ache of need.

Then he shifted lower.

He moved her thighs apart with his hands, letting them smooth across her skin. Shards of bliss jolted through her and settled in her inner core. His fingers caressed and teased. It had been too long since she'd felt his touch. She couldn't wait any longer.

Her need was too great.

She reached down and grabbed his shoulders. She pulled him closer. Catal inhaled sharply and then lifted her to him. He watched her face as he entered her with a slow, steady motion. She closed her eyes and savored each delicious sensation that spread through her as inch by inch he slid into her. When he filled her completely, he paused.

She opened her eyes and smiled. "It's like coming home after a long exile. How could I have lived without this?"

"You won't have to ever again." Catal pulled back and thrust deep. "I will always be here for you, as long as you desire me."

A shiver of delight raced through her. "That will be forever."

All thought ceased as Catal continued to stroke within her. The tight spiral of tension that had been building was close to the edge. She lost herself in the joy of joining with the one man who completed her. Together, they moved with a rhythm that their bodies remembered until they both exploded into ecstasy.

They shuddered with the aftermath of their lovemaking.

Catal gathered Selena close.

She cuddled into Catal's chest. "I missed you."

"Every day you were in my thoughts." Catal pulled the sheets over them. "A Hunter only bonds once. Our myths told of the despair he would feel if he was parted from his mate. The truth is worse than the legends."

Selena kissed his chest. "Never again. We must promise each other to always discuss our concerns."

"No matter what we have to talk about, or however painful it might seem, nothing could be as bad as these years apart."

She looked up at him and marveled that he was here with her. It was as if a light had been switched on. She basked in the brilliance of its glow now. With Catal by her side, she could face anything. She reached up and touched his stubble roughened jaw. He hadn't thought about anything but saving Tarrin and Gates these past few days.

"I love you." She blinked back the tears in her eyes. "I don't ever want to be parted from you again."

He bent and brushed his lips across hers. "I will want only you for the rest of my life. You and Tarrin are the only things that matter to me."

"You can't forget you're a Hunter."

"No." He gazed at her with unblinking eyes. "But I will give it up for you."

"You'll walk away?"

"If that's what you need." Catal kissed her forehead. "I am bonded to you. You are the only thing that matters. These past years have been hell. I can't go through that again."

"You won't have to."

Selena put her hand on his chest. His heart beat at a frantic pace. It beat only for her. For the first time, she really understood what that meant. He would walk away from his brothers if that was what she needed. At one time she had abhorred everything he stood for. Now she knew better.

Catal stood for honor and justice.

"I could never ask you to turn your back on who you are." Selena inhaled and looked up at him. "Loving someone means accepting everything about them."

Catal frowned. "You hate violence."

"I love you." Selena's voice's was a low whisper. "You help others. I see that now."

"I haven't always been on the right side of the law. That won't change in the future."

"You were always a Hunter." Selena kissed his chest. "Even when you worked for my brother, your unit didn't do everything he ordered."

"It was against the Sacred Code." Catal's tone was puzzled.

"That's what I mean." Selena smiled up at him. "Despite all of the horrors humans put you through, you still respected your code. You didn't harm women or children. You still had honor."

Catal swallowed. "You don't hate me for hiring out as a mercenary?"

Selena shook her head. "You had few choices."

"What does this mean for us?"

"You are a Hunter." Selena kissed his chin. "You fight for righteousness and that is a noble cause. I am proud of you."

Catal exhaled. "So you don't want me to leave the others?"

"No. I love the man you are today." Selena stroked up his chest. "I loved the man you were before, but I was too young to understand what that meant."

"I didn't believe that I was bonded either." Catal shuddered. "By Cygnus and Warrior, I cannot lose you again."

"So many wasted years." Selena felt tears prick her eyes.

"Nothing was wasted. We learned how precious the gift of our bonding is."

Catal pulled her close and captured her lips. A fiery heat pulsed through her. His fingers framed her face and chin sending delicious jolts of sensation racing across her skin. He increased the pressure of his lips and she opened for him. The feel and smell of him was intoxicating. He had always been ready to make love. She reached out and stroked his hardened manhood.

A shiver of delight pulsed through her.

Catal never disappointed.

She'd been too innocent to realize how rare that was, but now she knew better. In the past, they had made love all night long. Molten heat settled in her womb at the thought of his stamina. She ached to feel him deep within her again.

"Love me." Her voice was husky with desire.

"Always."

Catal held her hands above her head and then brushed his lips over hers. She arched her body toward him, but he moved to the side. His free hand stroked and fondled her breasts. She trembled as exquisite bliss flooded her senses. Anticipation and yearning throbbed within her.

"I intend to pleasure you all night long." His voice was low and seductive.

His tongue darted between her lips and slid over hers. She moaned and curled her tongue around his, savoring each delightful stroke. By the time his lips moved away, a restless heat suffused her body. His mouth roamed lower, nipping and soothing along her neck until he reached her breasts.

His tongue flicked across a nipple, tasting and licking before taking it into his mouth and sucking. A jolt of intense rapture vibrated every nerve in her body. Tension coiled and tightened within her.

She was on the edge of climax.

She arched her hips, begging Catal for the release she craved. Instead, he moved to her other breast and repeated his ministrations. Her head thrashed from side to side as the taunt spiral of pleasure became almost unbearable. Only then did Catal enter her.

His penetration triggered a shudder of ecstasy that exploded into bliss.

He continued to move within her as she reached fulfillment time and again. Only when she was completely satiated did she feel Catal shake with his own release.

She must have slept.

She surfaced from what felt like a fog, to feel Catal's fingers stroking the sensitive skin on her inner thigh. His lips were a light caress against her neck. She shivered as a spark of excitement came to life again. She felt boneless with satisfaction, but she couldn't deny the hunger Catal's touch caused.

"You're insatiable."

"I have eight years of loving to make up for."

Who was she to argue with a man on a mission?

She surrender to his expert touch, letting herself get lost once again in his lovemaking.

Chapter 20

They reached the reservation late in the afternoon of the next day. Catal had driven non-stop from the hotel. When they arrived at the house, Niail's mate, Kimi, had shown Selena the room that they would be staying in. Selena was exhausted and was now sleeping. Catal felt a twinge of guilt because he'd been the reason she hadn't slept the night before.

Ardal, and his mate Fiona, hadn't arrived yet.

He'd already heard from the other Hunters that all the children had been delivered safely to their homes. The last child was Gates, and Partlan was taking the boy home personally. The others were on their way to the reservation to meet up with Ardal. They'd arrive sometime tomorrow.

Catal surveyed the landscape of the reservation and relaxed. The air was clean and there was open space as far as you could see. Niail had assured him they would be safe, and Catal had to agree. No electricity or communication with the rest of the world offered an invisibility that was hard to find on this planet.

He felt right in his soul for the first time.

Selena was in his life, and her love made all of the anger he'd felt toward humans, dissipate. He'd been lucky to be able to witness Ardal and Fiona together. Ardal was the first Hunter to find his mate, and that's when Catal had learned that some humans were good. Selena's love had also taught him that anything was possible. There was one thing he had left to do.

He had to be honest with his son.

He had to tell Tarrin about his heritage.

"Are you and Mom going to stay together?"

Catal looked down at Tarrin and nodded. They were on the hill that was behind Kimi's house. They had a view of the road and driveway, but the pines hid them from sight. Tarrin had stayed close to him since they'd arrived in Montana. His voice held concern and Catal couldn't blame him. A lot had happened to him in the past week. He'd been kidnapped, sold, shot at, and learned he had a father. Now Catal had to tell him the rest of the story.

"Your mother knows I didn't betray her." Catal sat on a fallen log and motioned for Tarrin to sit beside him. "She feared that I had lied to her, so she left me. I have spent several years trying to find her."

"Couldn't you talk to her with your mind?"

"One day I will be able to, but the bond between us hadn't grown that strong when she left me." Catal cleared his throat. "A Hunter can only mind connect with a human if they are pair bonded."

Tarrin frowned. "Mom never told me anything about you."

"Your mother wanted to forget me." Catal looked up at the blue sky and sighed. "She was afraid to trust me because I am a Hunter."

"You said I was one too." Tarrin picked at the bark on the log. "Will that mean people will be afraid of me?"

"Your mother was frightened because I didn't tell her about myself."

"She asked you for help to find me, though." Tarrin grinned up at him. "I'm glad she did."

"So am I. You will find that others will come to you for aid." Catal eased his breathing. "It is wonderful to make things right for them, but there is danger, also."

"Like fighting bad people?"

Catal nodded. "There are others on this planet that will chase you because you are different."

Tarrin's eyes pulled together and his mouth pursed. "You mean because I can hear you in my head?"

"That is a secret among Hunters." Catal forced his voice to remain calm. "You may only speak of it amongst us. If others knew about it, they would hunt us down even more than they do now."

"I will keep it a secret." Tarrin's voice was serious. "Who are these people?"

"They work for government agencies on Earth." Catal pushed back his memories of the underground facilities where he had been imprisoned. "They do not want us here."

"Where should we be?"

"This is where you were born, but I was born on another planet."

There was a moment of silence before Tarrin spoke. "Are you from outer space?"

"I crash landed on this planet when I was ten years old." Catal looked down at his son. "I was hunted down and imprisoned. I was lucky to escape with my life."

"Why did they want you?"

"We weren't from Earth." Catal grimaced. "They were afraid we would hurt them, but we were only children and what they did to us was unspeakable. That is why I was afraid to trust humans. I never associated with them until I met your mother."

"Where are you from?" Tarrin's voice was hesitant.

"Since time began there have been Hunters." Catal began the history that was so familiar to him. "We were taken by the ancients to their planet Cygnus, to be their elite fighters. Genetic modification and training have made us the best warriors possible."

"So I am one too?"

"Yes, but you are unique." Catal touched his son's head. "In the past, we have been created in labs and birthing chambers. Never before has a Hunter been born of a woman. You are the first."

"Didn't you want mothers?" Tarrin's voice was puzzled.

"On Cygnus, no one has a mother. All children are brought into the world by birthing chambers." Catal lifted the sleeve of his left arm to show the two symbols marked there. He pointed to the first. "This signifies the day I was created and this is my clan. I am clan Saidir, as are you."

"What does Saidir mean?"

"We are the soldiers."

For the first time, he realized how much he had to teach Tarrin. He'd been three when he'd learned the differences between the clans. He was proud to be clan Saidir. They were always at the beginning of a battle and their skills allowed them quick reaction times and dexterity to manoeuver their weapons and bodies.

"Some Hunters are experts in healing, or in explosives, or in mechanical machines. Clan Saidir are fierce fighters and that's why we're chosen to go into battle first. Today, you will meet Ardal. He is clan Rioge. He is the leader."

"Is he scary?" Tarrin's voice held awe.

Catal smiled. He remembered the first time he'd met Ardal. They had just rescued him from a military secret base in northern Canada. Even surrounded by a group of armed Hunters, Ardal had faced them down. He was a leader beyond compare.

"No. Ardal is a friend and a true Hunter. He accepted me into his unit even though I threatened him and his mate."

"Why would you do that?" Tarrin moved closer to Catal.

Catal put his arm on his son's shoulder. "When I was left on Earth I was only ten years old and my training was incomplete. Ardal understood this and has helped us finish our teachings. He has great honor."

"Why did he come to Earth?" Tarrin leaned against Catal.

"He and his unit were sent here to be executed. They were the last Hunters in the universe. When they took over the ship that was transporting them to their death, it crashed on Earth."

"You mean they were to be killed?" Tarrin's voice shook. "Did they do something wrong?"

"There was a civil war on Cygnus and the Kaladin, who all Hunters obeyed, were defeated by the Holman. The Holman didn't trust us to follow their directives, so they ordered all Hunters killed. Ardal and his unit were the personal guards for the High Council. Their last mission was to hide the council and that's why they arrived back on Cygnus after the others had been executed."

"That's not right."

"A lot of things aren't just, that's why there are Hunters. We right the wrongs." Catal squeezed Tarrin closer.

"Like you did with those men who kidnapped Gates and me?"

"Exactly."

Tarrin was silent for a few minutes and then he spoke. "How long have you and the others been on Earth?"

"I have been here thirty years." Catal looked down at Tarrin. "Ardal and his unit have been here for ten months. I have learned much since I joined them, including that the legend about Hunters and their mates is true."

Tarrin looked up at his father. He gazed at him with a steady calm. "You didn't believe Mom was your mate."

"I knew that she was the only woman I had ever desired, but I didn't trust the legends." Catal felt a surge of pride. His son understood quickly. "Because of the modifications that were done to make us superior warriors, we develop a strong bond with only one woman. She is our pair bond. If we mate, it is an attachment that lasts for life. There will never be anyone else for me but your mother."

Catal suppressed the pain that shot through him at the thought of the years he'd spent apart from Selena. Tarrin was too young to understand the intensity of the pair bond. Because he was half human he might never experience it fully. That would be a loss. Tarrin might not have the pain of separation, but he would never experience the pleasure and oneness with a pair bond.

"What happened to the mates of the other Hunters? Were they left on Cygnus?"

"We were forbidden to mate."

Catal's voice was matter of fact. He knew that the Kaladin had denied them a great joy, but it was his own fault that he had lost Selena. If he'd been honest about who he was from the beginning, she would have trusted him.

Just then a sound from the road caught his attention. He focused and saw a dark van approaching the house. The others were here. He stood and reached a hand down for Tarrin.

"Ardal is here."

The two walked down from the hill to the house below.

Selena met them at the door. "They're in the kitchen."

Catal pulled her close and kissed her. "Let's go."

Ardal was standing at the kitchen counter. His arms were crossed across his chest and he looked formidable. Catal glanced at Tarrin to see how he was holding up. He was looking at the leader with wide eyes. Catal could understand why. Clan Rioge were larger than clan Saidir, but Ardal was an honorable leader. A man to be respected.

He held Selena close to his chest with one arm and his other hand was on Tarrin's shoulder. He stopped in front of Ardal. "This is my mate Selena, and our son, Tarrin."

Ardal nodded at Selena. "I am Ardal, of the clan Rioge, and last leader of the Hunters. I am honored to meet you." He then crouched down in front of Tarrin. "I hope we can be friends. We are brothers, so there is no need to fear me."

There was silence for a few seconds and then Tarrin smiled. "You can talk in my head too."

Ardal grinned. "All Hunters can speak to each other this way. Just focus and connect with me."

Tarrin frowned and his eyes narrowed. A couple of seconds later Ardal laughed and stood. He touched Tarrin's shoulder and glanced at Catal.

"Your father is an excellent warrior. He will do most of your training. After that, I will gladly help you learn." Ardal shook his head. "You are truly a miracle. One that no Hunter ever expected."

At that moment, Ardal's mate, Fiona, came in with Niail and Kimi. She was still as beautiful as Catal remembered. Her face glowed and her smile was welcoming. Niail and Kimi stood back as Fiona rushed into Ardal's arms.

"This is my mate and wife Fiona." Ardal introduced her to Selena and Tarrin. "She's been anxious to meet you."

"I'm so happy not to be the only woman in this group of men." Fiona sighed and then pushed away from Ardal. "Kimi has introduced me to her children Wil and Peta. They're adorable. Now there is Tarrin."

She hugged Tarrin. "I'm glad to see you're safe."

Tarrin nodded. "My father and the other Hunters saved us."

"I hear you were very brave and were able to help in your rescue." Fiona stood away and looked at him. "Would you like to go and play with Wil and Peta for a little while? Wil told me they've got a new board game."

Tarrin nodded and let Fiona lead him away. Niail pulled out a few of the kitchen chairs and motioned for the others to take a seat. Catal let Selena sit and then stood behind her with one hand on her shoulder. He sensed she was nervous meeting so many at once, so he sent her calm and peace. In time, she would come to trust the others. All Hunters had vowed to protect the mates of their brothers, so she had no reason to fear.

"You have recovered Niail?" Catal knew that Niail had suffered head injuries recently.

"I can connect again." Niail smiled as he sat beside Kimi. "If Kimi and the children had not rescued me, I would not be here."

"I'd say you saved us." Kimi gave Niail a kiss. "You put your life on the line for the children and me."

Fiona came back into the kitchen and sat on the chair Ardal held out for her. She waited for Ardal to sit and then took his hand in hers. Catal sensed that this gathering was more than an interest to meet Kimi and Selena.

"I haven't been feeling well for the last couple of months." Fiona's voice was low. "At first I thought that I was overtired with all the moving around we'd been doing since the crash. Then I began to suspect it was something more natural."

Selena cleared her throat. "Are you pregnant?"

"Yes." Fiona smiled. "It shouldn't be possible. Ardal is not from Earth. He wasn't even certain that the capability to have children hadn't been bred out of him. That's why I was excited when I heard about Tarrin."

"Niail looks human as do all the other Hunters." Kimi's voice held concern. "My grandfather thinks that they might be related to those who left Earth with the Star People eons ago."

"Your grandfather may be right." Kimi glanced over at Ardal who nodded. "When I found out I was pregnant the doctor in me was concerned about how our two species could create a child. I still have friends in the medical community, so I contacted one who agreed to do a DNA test on Ardal."

Catal frowned. "I don't understand what you were looking for."

"We know that animals of different species can have children together, but those offspring are rarely able to have babies."

"You mean like a horse and donkey creating a mule?" Selena's voice shook. "Are you saying that Tarrin might be sterile?"

Fiona reached over and clasped Selena's hand. "That was my fear too, but I was wrong. The DNA profile I had done on Ardal was a pleasant surprise."

"In what way?"

Catal had never given the mechanics of having children much thought. He hadn't believed that Hunters could mate, and children were not something that anyone had on Cygnus. Until Selena had told him that Tarrin was his son, he wouldn't have imagined it was possible. He could understand Fiona's concern when she found out she was pregnant.

"Ardal's DNA is human."

There was complete silence for several seconds. Niail was the first to speak. "How is that possible?"

"Either the inhabitants of Cygnus are humans, or you were from Earth originally." Fiona shrugged. "I have no other explanation."

"Grandfather knew." Kimi's voice was a low whisper. "He'd said that you were returning home."

"There is evidence of the genetic modifications though." Fiona pursed her lips. "The human genome has been mapped and there are long sequences of genes that are non-coding, in other words they don't produce proteins. In the past we called them junk DNA, but now we know that these sequences help with enhancing other genes, or regulating when a gene is switched on or off."

Catal frowned. "These are the areas where the modification have happened?"

"Yes." Fiona nodded. "You produce the same proteins as us, but you might make more of a protein for muscle mass than a normal human does."

"We are the same, yet different." Ardal crossed his arms. "I suspect that each clan has different modifications. This would explain the clan's expertise in certain areas."

"So essentially I am the same as Kimi, but I have modifications that make me stronger and a better shot." Niail's voice was hesitant.

Fiona nodded. "That's what we believe. I would have to have a sample of your blood to verify it."

"What about Tarrin?" Selena leaned forward. "How will he be different?"

"He would be like any other human baby. Half of his genes come from you and half from Catal."

"So he gets his ability to mind connect from a gene that Catal has passed on." Selena raised an eyebrow. "So there is no means of knowing what our children might inherit from their fathers."

"If Tarrin is any indication, I'd say he has inherited a lot from his father."

Catal was stunned by what he'd heard. He wasn't a scientist, but Fiona had given him a lot to think about. Tarrin was a Hunter, there was no doubt. The difference was that he would have a choice of whether he wanted to be a warrior or not. There was still one thing that bothered him.

"Why were our ancestors taken by the Kaladin?" Catal leaned close to the table.

"My grandfather said that the Star People asked the best warriors to join them." Kimi's voice was low. "Perhaps the Kaladin are the Star People of my grandfather's legends."

"It is very possible." Ardal shifted in his chair so that he was facing Kimi. "Since crashing on Earth, we have learned that many of our myths are true. There is no reason that the same is not true for your people's legends."

"Grandfather's teachings are very ancient." Kimi looked over at Niail. "If the Star People did take humans, they did it eons ago."

"Hunters have existed since time began according to the Kaladin." Niail frowned. "This might also be the reason Earth was the planet we were heading toward."

"And why we were sent here for training." Catal crossed his arms.

He pushed away his anger. For years he had blamed the humans for what they had done to him. To find out that he was one of them would take some getting used to. He needed time to understand and come to terms with what had happened to him. Right now, all he wanted was to make certain that his son did not suffer as he had.

"Earth is more our home than we realized." Ardal's voice was calm. "We must not forget our training or the Sacred Codes. We are still Hunters."

"We have traveled much of the universe." Niail spoke in a quiet voice. "Our experience and breeding means we will stand apart."

"But we belong here." Catal frowned. "This is probably why we have found mates here also."

Ardal nodded. "This is true. I am only surprised that the others who crashed here with you, did not find mates. Perhaps your implants were still working."

"Something must have happened to mine." Catal rubbed the scar on his arm where his implant had been removed. "I had never been attracted to a human before I met Selena."

"Tell us about that." Ardal leaned back in his chair. "When we first met, you did not believe in the legend of mates."

"I was afraid to admit it." Catal looked down at Selena and stroked a finger down her cheek. "I hadn't trusted that it was a pair bonding. Instead, I believed that I had betrayed my brothers by being with a human woman."

"Understandable considering what happened to you on Earth." Ardal sighed. "This may be hard for those of you who were stranded here as children to deal with. For too many years, Lorcan and the rest of the clan Saidir have seen humans as the enemy."

"It will take time." Catal sighed. "They will have a better understanding of the work they do to bring justice to others."

"Instead of hiring out as mercenaries."

Selena shuddered. "Even when I thought that Catal had betrayed me, I still worried that he might be dead somewhere because of the work he did."

"That still might happen." Catal's voice was serious. "We are honor bound to help, whether it is a dangerous situation or not."

"I understand, but a part of me believes that as long as you are fighting for justice, you will be protected."

"Let's hope." Kimi's voice was low.

"I protect my men as much as possible." Ardal's voice was firm. "The crash and the Holman took too many of our brother's lives. I cannot lose another man."

"That's enough sad talk." Fiona stood up. "I think it's time we celebrate. Niail is better, Catal has found his mate and son, and we're going to have a baby."

"Do you know what it is yet?" Kimi pushed away from the table.

Fiona shook her head. "I want to be surprised."

"I will warn you that you may need help with the delivery." Selena stood. "Tarrin was too large for me to have naturally."

Fiona bit her lip. "I've already considered that and have made plans to be near a hospital close to my due date."

"When will that be?" Selena walked away from him and joined Kimi and Fiona.

The women went into the living room, but their excited voices could be heard in the kitchen. Their pair bonding with a Hunter made them fugitives, but none of that seemed to concern them. Catal wasn't sure if Selena realized how difficult life in hiding would be. He would make certain that she was safe.

He vowed to protect her with his life.

He turned to Ardal.

He was frowning.

"You will learn that women love discussing babies." Catal grinned.

"I have not seen this before." Ardal shook his head.

"Fiona has only been with you." Niail's voice was dry. "Kimi is frequently talking with her friend Ann for hours at a time."

"Has being a father been difficult?" Catal's voice was serious.

"They have been very tolerant of my mistakes." Niail shook his head. "There is so much we do not know about children. For the first time in my life I feel uncertain."

"I understand." Catal leaned against the counter. "I never fear for myself, but now I worry about Selena and Tarrin."

"It makes the life of a warrior more difficult." Ardal heaved a sigh.

"It makes it worthwhile, though." Catal remembered the passion and love he'd shared with Selena. Tarrin was a miracle that their bonding had made possible.

"True." Ardal pushed back from the table. "I would not wish it any other way."

"Nor would I." Niail stood up and followed Ardal.

Catal walked into the living room. Ardal and Niail had pulled their mates close, but the woman were still talking to each other. A surge of contentment flooded him at the sight of Selena relaxed and happy.

There was nothing he wouldn't do for her. To have her back in his life was more than he had ever dreamed possible. All those years of pain and loneliness were over. No more would he have to wonder if she'd been real, if the love they'd shared had ever happened. They were bonded.

Selena was his mate.

She would be near always.

Selena looked at him and smiled. The world righted itself in that moment. All the pain of his childhood was healed. He was home now.

Author's Note

When I studied biology in the early eighties, the decoding of DNA, deoxyribonucleic acid, the genetic building block of living organisms on Earth, had progressed enough that my professors were discussing the possibility of mapping the complete human genome one day. At the time, I remember thinking that would take forever to accomplish. I was wrong.

By 2003 the sequencing of the human genome was completed. This means that we are able to identify specific genes and their functions. Some areas of DNA do not produce proteins, so are considered non-coding sequences. Initially, it was thought that these areas had no function, but time and research has shown that these sequences enhance or regulate other genes.

Today we can use DNA not only to find criminals, but also to trace our ancestors. Knowing the sequencing of our genes allows us to understand how to change those genes. The possibilities for genetic manipulation and engineering are endless. Already there are discussions of allowing human trials of an In Vitro Fertilization technique that would combine the DNA of three people to ensure that disease causing mutations will not be passed on to children.

As I look ahead to the future I can envision a world where genetic engineering will wipe out diseases such as diabetes, mitochondrial disease, or hemophilia. At the same time, there are ethical and moral considerations that society will have to deal with. Questions about whose DNA will be used for recombinant engineering, and whether people will be discriminated against because their genes could potentially cause diseases like cancer, need to be answered.

Science is already at the cutting edge of what used to be called fiction.

About the Author

Cynthia Clement began writing stories in her teens, but it wasn't until her forties that she became serious about writing. She lives in Canada with her husband of thirty years, her teenaged son, and two dachshunds. She has an eclectic range of interests including paranormal phenomena, ghost hunting, quilting, reading, gardening, and great conversation.

Her first book, The Seduction of Sarah, was a finalist in the HOLT Medallion Best First Book Category. Her novel aHunter4Rescue won first place in the Paranormal Category of the 2014 International Digital Awards. Her books, whether historical, paranormal, or science fiction, all focus on love, honor, and suspense. To find out more information about her writing and books or to sign up for her newsletter please visit her website www.cynthiaclement.com

Available Books

aHunter4Hire Series

aHunter4Rescue
aHunter4Saken
aHunter4Life
aHunter4Ever

Historical Romances

The Seduction of Sarah
The Seduction of Madalyn
Pleasuring Emily
Christmas Kisses

Coming Soon

Her Shadow Lover

www.ingramcontent.com/pod-product-compliance
Lightning Source LLC
Chambersburg PA
CBHW051821170626

46807CB00003B/972